FINDING GRACE

B. E. BAKER

Addy really needs a raise, like yesterday. Thanks to a mountain of school debt, she's heartily sick of being broke. So when she discovers she's being considered for a promotion? She's GIDDY.

Until she finds out that she needs to bring in accounts of her own, or she doesn't stand a chance.

Unfortunately, the only person she knows who might need a PR company is her ex from high school. She'd *almost* rather die than ask for his business, especially given the mess he's created. But when she finally steels up her nerve and asks Ben if her company can help, she realizes that she's in trouble.

Many things have changed since high school, but their chemistry isn't one of them. It's as explosive as it ever was. Can Addy remember all the reasons things didn't work the first time around? Or is history doomed to repeat itself?

ADDY

s a kid, I spent more time clipping coupons than I did watching cartoons. Mom kept us on a tight budget, as in, we couldn't afford a pack of gum, tight. It motivated me to study hard, work doggedly, and focus so I wouldn't have to live in such a miserly way.

I worked part time for all four years of college, found the best-paying jobs I could every summer and holiday break, and I only took four days off between graduation and my first day of work. I told myself that once I graduated and started making money, I'd pay things off in no time. That's when I'd live the good life—finally.

But I've worked full time for four years now, and I'm still flat broke.

After taxes and FICA come out—*what the heck is FICA, anyway?*—my paycheck barely covers my rent, my utilities, and my student loans. It leaves me with $885 each month for everything else I need. Food? Toothpaste? Toilet paper? Fast food? Yep, all of that comes out of the same tiny pile.

Depressingly, I've only saved $711 in the four years I've

been working for the Princeton Public Relations Lab. I actually really enjoy my job—I just need it to pay more.

"Next Friday!" My friend Elana's voice when she's excited and reining it in is all high and squeaky. Like a Labrador retriever squeezing a tennis ball. "*Next Friday* they're announcing which two account executives are being promoted to account supervisor."

It's a big promotion. . .and more importantly, it comes with a healthy pay raise. "Twelve days." I groan. It's too soon, and it's too far away. How can it be both? "Do you know whether they've already decided?"

Elana scoots toward me, the wheels of her rolling office chair whizzing, crowding into my tiny cubicle. "For one of them, yeah."

She's talking about Victoria Marino, the granddaughter of our President of Client Services. She's gorgeous, she's brilliant, and she's ridiculously lazy. "It's so unfair." I'm careful to keep my voice low. Grumbling about nepotism is a fast track to nowhere. No one seems to be paying any attention to us, but working in a fishbowl makes it hard to know for sure.

Elana's voice is the faintest whisper. "I hear they've narrowed the other slot down to two top candidates." She always does this—buries the lead. She thinks it's charming. Usually, it makes me want to strangle her, even though she's my closest work friend. This time, though, I'm desperate for the information her adept social skills have uncovered.

"And?"

"Yvette." Her head whips the same direction as mine —toward the far wall. Yvette Morris is *the worst*. She reigns over her tiny corner of the office with total confidence, dispensing advice and condescension in equal measure.

"She has been here five years," I grudgingly admit. She started a full year before I did.

But I work so much harder.

Long nights. Early mornings. Working from home. I take calls when they come in, sacrificing my plans to do whatever needs doing.

"You also take the hardest cases, and the ones no one wants. If you were a plumber, you'd be taking all the busted septic pipes and broken toilets." Elana shrugs. "That's probably why Lucas said that the other person being considered. . .is you."

She did it again—saved that information for the end. All the air whooshes out of my lungs, making it almost impossible to get my words out. "Me? Are you sure?"

Elana bobs her head, and the corner of her mouth quirks upward. "Why do you think I rushed over?" She pulls a Snickers out of her pocket. "I was saving this for that mid-afternoon lull, when my blood sugar drops low and all I want is a nap. But I figure I should split it with you now as a mini-celebration." She doesn't even wait to ask if I want half—I always want half of any kind of chocolate.

"But there's no way they'll pick me between the two of us." Yvette already acts and dresses like a supervisor. She's a year ahead of me.

"It would help if you stopped wearing high heels you stole from your *grandma*." Elana hands me half the Snickers.

I tuck my feet, encased in blocky black heels with a fair share of scuffs and dings, underneath my chair. "I'm sure they're not making decisions based on our clothing."

"It's a *Public Relations* firm," Elana says. "Of course they're basing it on how you present yourself. Duh."

"She's right, though." Harriet slides past Elana and perches on the edge of my desk.

My heart hammers in my chest—at least it was only Harriet who overheard us. She's the director I've worked with the most and my only friend in management, really. "Your intel is good." She nods at Elana. "But you missed the critical point."

My throat feels dry, so I clear it. "Which is?" The Snickers is starting to melt in my hand, but I can't very well stuff it in my mouth now, and I don't have anywhere else to put it. I shift my hand so she can't see it.

"I wasn't strictly authorized to share this with you." Her shoulders hunch and her voice drops a hair. "But we all agreed you're the better choice. You handle difficult things with grace, and you work harder than anyone else. Those two things alone would have secured you a promotion if you were going up against anyone but Yvette."

"I don't get it. She's not that hard working," Elana says. "Why is it a toss-up?"

"She brings in business," Harriet says. "Quite a lot of it, for a plain Jane account exec." She flips her hair. "And by our count, you've brought. . .exactly one client."

She doesn't mention that the client I brought was neither lucrative nor glamorous. It was also more of a fluke that I brought them over.

The grooming place where I take my Pomeranian, Foxy, used muzzles. It's kind of standard practice. Who takes their pet to a groomer if they're easy to brush? It's mostly the snarling, snapping, biting dogs that need to go to professionals, so, muzzles are kind of necessary. But a pet owner caught one of their employees screaming at a dog—it was pretty bad. They almost went out of business when clients all started dropping. As a Hail Mary, they called me and I did the whole case myself and applied the optional thirty percent family and friends discount.

"One of the important things a supervisor does is manage the account executives and interface with existing and prospective clients. But another important task is being able to grow our client roster. If she can do that more effectively, then. . ."

"You're saying that unless I bring in more clients, I'll stay where I am?"

Harriet shrugs. "That's basically the answer, yeah. It's not personal, but you're only doing one half of what you need to do in order to succeed here."

"How much time do I have?"

She shrugs. "This week, if you want to be safe. They don't wait to make the decision until the day they announce it." She spins on her heel and walks toward the private offices.

"Easy," Elana says. "Just magically bring in crap tons of money."

I snort. "Right? Gosh, if only it had occurred to me to contact some of my über rich friends before now."

"Yvette's parents are realtors and they move a lot of houses. That means they meet a lot of people. I hear all her referrals have come from them."

Meanwhile, my mom's the assistant manager at a grocery store, and I haven't seen my dad since my brother Scott dumped an entire bucket of paint on my stepmom's brand new rug at Christmas more than a decade ago. "I'm totally screwed."

Elana doesn't even argue with me. She likes the idea of having a friend who's a supervisor, but it's just not realistic, apparently. I sigh dramatically. "How am I ever supposed to replace my grandma shoes when I'm stuck eating ramen the last week of every month?"

"Maybe you stop going out to lunch the first two weeks of every month. Then you'd have enough left over to eat something nice, like a peanut butter sandwich."

We both laugh at that one.

I say, "I'd rather deal with the lows than never enjoy the highs."

Harriet walks back over, glaring at Elana as she approaches. "Your hovering isn't helping her." She drops a newspaper on my desk. "If you don't have any connections to play on, search through that."

"I didn't even realize they still printed those." I glance at the title, *The Atlanta Journal-Constitution*. That's about as pretentious sounding as it gets.

"Old people like me still like to read on paper." Harriet pauses. "When I was in your shoes—"

"You wore old, clunky grandma shoes too?" Elana asks.

"Old and worn? Yes." Harriet's face softens. "I had no one powerful or important to help me find clients, but they expect you to bring people to the table. I cold-called hundreds of people before I got lucky, but it could have happened at any time."

"But how does a newspaper help?" Elana asks.

"They don't report on kittens and rainbows," Harriet says. "Most of the companies and people mentioned in this paper will need some help."

She's brilliant.

"Now get to work, Elana, and let Addy start making some calls."

The front-page article is on toxic mold, but the damage isn't anyone's fault in particular and unless there's some kind of mold federation, there's no one to pay for our services. I don't have to look very far to find something promising, though. On the front of page two, above the fold, a gorgeous face that I'll never forget stares back at me.

·   ·   ·

NEWBERG AUTO REPAIR IN MAJOR DISREPAIR

The office manager of Newberg Auto's corporate office, located in Centennial Hill, filed sexual harassment charges today against Benjamin Newberg. Faith Johnson alleges that the owner of the large and prosperous Atlanta auto repair chain lured her to engage in sex acts with monetary incentives and coerced her when such measures failed. She claims that such behavior was ongoing—lasting more than a year. It wasn't until she became pregnant and he insisted on an abortion that she decided to take legal action.

The local magistrate found preliminary evidence compelling enough to set the case for trial. Ms. Johnson is represented by Axel, Knorr, and Hoff. When we reached out, Mr. Newberg had no comment, and his wife also refused to give a statement, but when our staff went by four different locations, business was booming. It appears that, so far, there have been no ramifications for what appears to be wholesale sexual misconduct.

For almost ten years, Ben Newberg, with his broad, winning smile, his track star physique, and his perfectly streaked blond hair has been 'the one that got away.' I try to suppress the twinge of jealousy I feel over him having a wife, because it's ridiculous. Why would I be jealous of that poor woman?

I'm glad he dumped me back then—how much worse would my life be now if *I'd been the one who* married him? I tear off the page and fold it up to show my mom.

"Ooh, you found one?" Elana's peering around the edge of our cubicle divider.

I shake my head. "Nah. Just turns out this guy I used

to have a crush on in high school is a much bigger loser than I thought."

"Whoa, something bad happened to someone you know?" Her eyes widen. "Isn't that *exactly* what you need?"

I blink. "To feel better about losing, you mean?"

"No, that's a connection, girlfriend. And you better use it."

ADDY

There is absolutely no chance that I'm going to march into Ben Newberg's office, say, 'Hey! Remember me? The girl you flirted with, took on one date, and then dumped?'

I shake my head. "I don't have a connection. It's more like a broken power line or something."

"Girl. What did you think connections *are*? No one has people standing around, begging to help them out." She laughs. "It's someone you know, and when something bad happens, you're there, offering to help."

"This isn't someone I know. I *knew* him, back in like, 10th grade, for a few weeks. We haven't spoken a single time since."

She snatches the paper out of my hand and unfolds it. "Oh my gosh, look at that jawline." Her mouth drops open. "Actually forget the jaw. Look at those eyes." She looks up at me, her fingers crumpling the paper. "This guy you don't know is super hot." She bites her lip.

"Did you even read the article?"

Her eyes focus and scan downward. "Whoa, a sex

scandal?" She drops the paper on my desk. "Who needs a promotion. Just let him rot."

But I really do need a promotion, and someone is going to get his money. It might as well be us, right?

Would the fact that he knew me a long time ago help me to get this horrible job? I mean, the last thing I want to do is bail out someone like this—or save his company. But I chose PR. This is kind of a big part of what we do, helping people improve their image when they've screwed something up royally.

Before I can second guess anymore, I search the company directory online, pick up my office phone, and dial.

"Newberg Auto Repair Corporate," a woman's voice says. "How may I direct your call?"

"Ben Newberg." My hands tremble as I force the words out.

"He's not here," she says. "He's preparing for a press conference. And if this is about—"

"A press conference? Where and when is that?"

She rattles off the information—a hotel not far from their office—and I glance at my watch. I have an hour and forty minutes. It's just enough time to put together some preliminary ideas and a rough plan of action. I'm frantically slamming basic ideas onto a few diagrams and display maps when Elana bumps me.

"What?"

"I called your name three times, space cadet. What're you doing?"

"They're having a press conference, and I'm going to go pitch our firm's services to him."

"Who is this guy, anyway? An unlucky ex-boyfriend?"

I wish. Or, rather, now that I know the kind of person he is, maybe I don't wish. Er, I definitely don't wish. "He was pretty much the king of our high school."

"Really?"

I shrug. "Maybe not the king, but like an earl or a duke or something."

"Do you even know the difference between an earl and a duke?" Elana arches an eyebrow. She's never without a romance novel to read—most of them featuring shirtless men on the cover.

I figured she'd appreciate the reference. I guess not. "That's so not the point. He was super hot, rich, and a track star. He drove a brand new sports car *and* had a shiny black truck for outdoorsy stuff. And we met a long time ago, and I thought he liked me, but he never really did."

"You're missing the point. Which is, whether he will remember you."

"Unless he's done a *lot* of drugs in the intervening time, I'm sure he will." I wish that were a joke. I'd have put money on the fact that the Ben I knew would never have harassed anyone in a million years, much less solicited anyone or threatened them. So, clearly, I don't really know him either.

Elana starts shooting off pointers, and she takes it upon herself to put together two different scenario maps. Once we're done, she brushes off the lapels of my petal pink business suit coat. "You're going to march in there, leave this perverted loser's jaw dangling, and land this account." She beams. "And then you can fob him off on someone else if you want, but you're going to manage all my projects from here on out. Because next Friday, they'll announce you as the new manager, not Yvette."

I hope she's right.

Armed with my scenarios and my action plans, I hail a cab and head for The Omni at Centennial Park. I can't help thinking about the first time I ever spoke to Ben. He was so cool, so funny, and so handsome. He was so far out of my league that we weren't even playing in the same arena.

Even so, I'm still struggling to get my head around the idea that Ben Newberg would cheat. I just can't fathom it. He was so. . .upright.

In spite of the years that have passed, in spite of the way we left things, butterflies swarm round and round in my belly as the cab stops. There's a Ferris wheel to my left, on the park side of Marietta Street. If school weren't in session right now, I'm sure kids would be running all over the place, or standing in line and bouncing, waiting for their turn to climb up and float up high in the sky. As it is, the whole thing almost makes me sad. Like an imagined past that never happened, the amusement park is empty, almost forgotten.

"Lady?" the cab driver asks.

I need to focus on the here and now. "Right, sorry." I pay my fare, open the door, and step out onto the sidewalk leading to the glass-fronted Omni Hotel.

"He's a loser," I remind the butterflies. "He may be gorgeous, but he forced himself on a co-worker, a subordinate no less, and now he's paying for his disgusting behavior. Hopefully paying our firm."

A woman walking down the street looks at me sideways, her lips curled up in disgust. She could have just assumed I was on the phone. People do that—use headphones and just talk. But humans always assume the worst. The woman muttering on the sidewalk is clearly crazy. The man who was reported to be a disgusting jerk must really be.

That's a good reminder to me not to believe anything I've read without hearing both sides.

I square my shoulders and march through the front doors and into the spacious lobby. It takes me a moment, but I still have four minutes to spare when I find the right conference room and squeeze myself through the back door. Clearly not much is going on in Atlanta now, or a press conference for a sex scandal from a CEO of an auto repair chain wouldn't be this well attended.

I wonder if they chose this conference room on purpose—to ensure this stays brief. It's small, it's crowded, and it's far too warm. I shrug out of my light, early November jacket, and hang it over the chair I managed to claim near the back. Reporters are jostling each other in front of and to the side of me. They're murmuring, and consulting their notes.

That makes me the usurper here, clearly. I'm not looking for a way to torpedo him further—to my surprise I actually want to help him minimize the damage. I mean, occupationally, I should have wanted to do that all along. It's my job. But no matter what narrative I tell myself, I keep trying to figure out how some part of what I read could be untrue, how Ben could be less of a villain than he seems.

Maybe the woman, whom I usually side with automatically, is actually lying. Or could poor Ben have misread the signals and thought she was interested when she wasn't? Could he have been offering her a legitimate bonus or something, and she thought it was solicitation?

Or perhaps she's only jealous that he's not in love with her, and she retaliated with this.

Although—he is married. And he did get her pregnant. I need to stop trying to make him into the boy I remember.

Ugh.

Someone very tall taps on the microphone. When she turns, I realize it's a woman. "My name is Natasha Appenziel, and I'm the head of administration at Newberg Auto Repair. I'm here today, along with Ben Newberg, to address the allegations of Ms. Johnson. First, Mr.

Newberg will read a statement. Then afterward, he'll open to questions, but only for ten minutes."

I cringe a little, thinking about whether he has any plan at all. Why is he doing a press conference so early? Part of me hopes this gets much worse, because then they'll really need me. But the little girl inside of me, the one who has thought of Ben at least once a week for almost a decade, hopes that he'll be able to walk to the microphone and deny all the charges.

Easy peasy.

I would believe him.

Which is completely moronic.

When Natasha backs up, an even taller person who was formerly obscured by her frame walks toward the microphone. After he passes her, his face finally becomes clear.

As a teenager, Ben had this easygoing and still-somehow-shy charm. He was confident and talented, yet vulnerable. He had kind eyes that always sparkled with mischief. His sky blue eyes, his California surfer hair, and his stylish clothing, coupled with the miles and miles he ran each day, made him someone all the girls sighed over.

But the man who walks up to the microphone is not that self-assured teen.

He's taller. He's filled out—and even through the clean lines of his suit, his biceps bulge as he rests his hands on the top of the podium. His skin is that same tawny golden color it always was, but his eyes aren't boyish anymore. They're. . .a rogue's eyes. He's every bit as smart, as funny, and as mischievous, but now he's also something more.

He's cocky.

Which is exactly what I would expect of a dirty, disgusting philanderer. As his eyes scan the audience, his expression darkens, doubt entering in to dampen his typical confidence and charm. There are a lot of people ready to attack him, and I'm guessing he doesn't know any of them. It's part of my job to know most of the reporters in Atlanta, but only because getting them to report on things in certain ways is also something I do.

Normal people don't know reporters.

"Thank you for coming today," he says. "My name is Ben Newberg, and I understand that you've all gathered here to confront our company about the allegations made by Mrs. Johnson. First and foremost, I'd like to offer an apology, from all of us at Newberg Auto Repair. As many of you know, we have expanded in the past twenty years from forty or so locations in Atlanta, to three times that many, spreading as far north as Tennessee, and extending as far south as Florida. The reason our repair and tire shops have done so well is that we embrace a different mentality than most auto repair shops. Our goal is to fix your issues in the most cost-effective way possible—not to turn the largest profit. When people bring their cars to us, we don't simply tell them how much it would cost. We explain their problem, and then we give them options. They can repair. They can replace. They can delay. We partnered with a software company to gather data on the known problems cars face, and we've been able to give an almost entirely accurate window for each issue that shows the risk of delaying repairs until it's something you can afford to do."

"You sound like an advertisement," a man I don't know next to me shouts. "I'm not interested."

"Is it true? Did you pay someone to sleep with you?" Evangeline from Channel Three is holding a camera phone—looks like Stan couldn't make it for some reason. I wonder if they'll actually consider using any of that footage, or if it's just for verification purposes.

"Did you threaten to fire her if she didn't go to bed with you?" The man next to me is annoying even me.

"I'm not trying to advertise our services to the reporters here today," Ben says. "I'm merely stating our mission statement and purpose. And I told you I'd take questions once I was done. I volunteered to do this press conference, and I'd appreciate if you'd all be respectful of that."

There's a lot of grumbling, but no more shouted questions. I'm actually impressed with how he's handling them. He's not rude or aggressive, but he's not backing down, either.

"The principle on which we built our business," Ben says, "is still our principle going forward. None of the services or processes at any of our locations have changed." He inhales slowly. "But since the article in the Constitution released yesterday, our traffic has been cut in half in the locations I've spoken to in Atlanta. We imagine people are bothered by the allegations of Mrs. Johnson, and we certainly understand why."

"But did you—"

Ben holds up his hand, tension lines around his mouth clear even from here. "I'm nearly done."

After a little grumbling, the reporters settle down again.

"It is our official position that the mistakes made, which were personal relationship mistakes, by our top executives are not relevant when it comes to our business model. We would kindly ask if you would allow the matter to be resolved by the courts, as applicable, and between the parties involved." He nods. "That is all. As promised, I'll take questions for ten minutes."

I can barely remember my own name in the cacophony that ensues.

"Did you sleep with Mrs. Johnson?" the man next to me bleats.

"Was it consensual?" Evangeline asks.

"Was she forced?" Thom from Channel Eleven asks.

"Did you think she wanted to sleep with you?" Paul from the Herald shouts.

"Is she pregnant with your child?" I have no idea who's talking now.

"What does your wife think?" a very nasal voice demands.

Ben looks to his right, and then he looks to his left. The questions continue to bombard him.

They weren't this rude when they found *e coli* in that local place's ice cream.

"You should be ashamed of yourself," Oliver from the Star says. "Lying to your employees and forcing yourself on them isn't a 'relationship issue.' It's assault."

"Why do you need to coerce women at all?" the obnoxious man next to me asks. "You're a good-looking guy. If you want to cheat on your wife, just do it with someone who's willing."

"Enough!" I yell at the top of my lungs.

I have carefully cultivated relationships with most of these people over the past four years. Some of them don't know who I am, but most of them know and like me. Evangeline, in particular, actually looks a little embarrassed. Maybe she got carried away—I don't know. I've turned all my attention on Ben.

When his eyes meet mine, they widen. "Addy?"

I wondered whether he'd recognize me. "Mr. Newberg can't answer any questions unless you quiet down long enough for him to speak. How about you go one at a time? There's no prize for being the first one."

"Thank you," Ben says.

"Let's start with the most important question we all want answered," I say. "Did you sleep with Mrs. Johnson?"

"Me?" Ben frowns. "I most certainly did not."

Tension I didn't realize I was carrying around melts away after his utter and complete denial. "You didn't?"

"*I* never slept with Mrs. Johnson."

"If that's true, why would she claim you did?" Evangeline asks. "Is she pressuring your firm to give her money? Is she in debt?"

The tall woman who introduced him, Natasha something, steps in front of him, tapping the microphone. "There appears to be a misunderstanding, which all of you seem to share. Mrs. Johnson never even alleged that Ben Newberg—" She points. "—had any kind of relationship, inappropriate or otherwise, with her."

When I look around, the faces of the reporters and newspeople reflect the bafflement I'm feeling.

No one's alleging it? But. . . "The paper said—"

"Ben's father is named Ben*jamin* Newberg," Natasha says. "Ben Newberg, behind me, is not a junior. His full name is Ben. He doesn't even go in to the corporate office most days, and he barely knows Mrs. Faith Johnson at all."

That appears to be news to all of us.

And for the first time since I saw that newspaper article, I can take a deep breath again. My former crush, Ben, did nothing wrong. He could still be all the amazing things I remember.

The bad news is that I didn't even come up with scenarios that deal with his *dad*, the owner of the entire company, having an affair with someone half his age.

�֍ 3 ֍

ADDY

Ben makes a beeline for me the second the press conference ends. "You're a reporter now?"

It's a strange phrase—a beeline. Don't bees bobble all over the place? Wobbling and zipping and spinning? But in English, it means that someone goes somewhere directly.

"Addy?"

I hate when my brain does this, spinning around and buzzing. It happens whenever I'm flustered.

"Do you work for a newspaper now?" Ben's eyes are wide.

"I'm not a reporter."

He blinks. "But you're—"

"I actually didn't come for the press conference as much as I did to see if I could set up a meeting with you."

He frowns. "You work for an automotive company? Or maybe you're. . ." He trails off, clearly not understanding why in the world I would ask for a meeting.

"I'm an account executive with Princeton Public Relations Lab," I say. "I'm in PR."

He exhales. "Got it." His smile is wry. "I suppose that's a good reason to be here."

"Actually, it's a terrible reason. They should really tell the fresh-faced college kids who take their first public relations class on the very first day that their job will be to deal with clients who are in crisis, day in and day out. I wonder how many of us would have defected to marketing." I force a smile. Often humor defuses an otherwise tense situation. That's Public Relations 101. Knowing *when* to use humor and when to be deadly serious is, of course, Public Relations 201.

Judging by Ben's failure to laugh, I gauged that one a little wrong. We're probably still too close to ground zero for that joke to land.

"If you don't have time or interest in talking to a PR firm, that's totally fine." I can practically feel my best friend Mary jabbing me in the side and chiding me. *Be more assertive. Go for it—don't back down.* That's what she'd tell me. My friend Elana would agree, I'm sure. "But you shouldn't make that decision until you've at least heard what kinds of things we can do for Newberg Auto."

Not that my ideas are all applicable anymore.

"I won't lie and say this is how I hoped to see you again," Ben says. "But I do think that a public relations company is a good idea. I'm a little embarrassed I didn't think of it myself."

A perky woman with a spiky black hairdo spins on her heel. "Did you say a public relations company might be a good idea?" Her smile is 150 blazing watts. "I'm Beatrice Cooper, an account manager with Kimball PR. I'd be delighted to sit down with you and map out a plan to navigate this troubled time."

Ben quirks one eyebrow, his sky blue eyes icy. "Actually, we've already decided to go with Princeton, but thanks for your willingness."

My jaw drops.

"That woman set my teeth on edge," Ben whispers.

"I appreciate the vote of confidence," I say, "but you should hire the company that you feel will do the best job handling the crisis." I'm not sure why it annoys me that he's declining other PR companies. I should be giddy, but it feels wrong, somehow.

"No need to get flustered." Ben's smile this time is real, both dimples coming out to play. "I'll make you earn our business, don't worry."

"I'm not flustered," I lie. His smile always threw me, a fact that apparently the passing of almost ten years hasn't changed.

"Knowing me in high school didn't get you the meeting, if that's what upset you," he says. "It was the fact that you stood up and intervened when I choked up there. You shut the reporters down and focused the press conference on things that mattered."

"Not that any of this matters for an *auto repair* chain," I say. "And I think that's the point. We need to contain this until people can remember that as interesting as it may be to watch scandals unfold in their community, the behavior of Benjamin Newberg isn't really relevant to the service they'll receive on their car."

One of the reporters has caught wind of our conversation. "But don't you think *honesty* is relevant when choosing someone to work on your car?" He whips out a phone, presumably to record the answer. "If the leadership has proven they have terrible moral fiber, wouldn't that impact the public's ability to trust them?"

"We were just leaving." Ben's hand closes around my upper arm, his fingers as strong and steady as they ever were. A shiver runs down my spine, but I refuse to acknowledge it. He already said I was flustered, and I wouldn't want someone who was flustered and shaky to be in charge of my company's image.

"We were," I say.

It's a fine line between dragging someone out of a room and leading them out—but Ben walks it as well as he ever did. His hand loosens whenever I slow down, so that he's guiding, not yanking. Once we clear the outer doors, he releases me entirely.

I shouldn't be disappointed.

That's a stupid reaction to have—I know he's married. I saw the wedding announcement in the paper. I was having a *day*, and I even cried about it. The one that got away. Or ran away. Or perhaps 'the one that dumped me and ran'? That's the most accurate.

"Can you follow me to our corporate headquarters?" he asks. "I really would like to hear your ideas."

"If you're willing to wait for me to grab a cab, I'd be glad to," I say. "Or maybe there's a side room we can use here?"

"You came in a cab?" He smiles. "You can just ride with me, then."

"I can go through a few ideas on the way," I say. "That'll be the most time efficient."

His lips compress and his head tilts. "Are you in public relations, or are you an efficiency expert?"

"I'm respectful of my clients' time." If I'm a little defensive, well, he seems to be mocking me and I don't appreciate it. "I'd think that was a good thing."

"It is good." He starts walking, leaving me to trot after him like a dutiful dog.

With his stupidly long legs, he moves really fast. I'm practically jogging to keep up. It's a relief when we reach the elevator bay.

For about three seconds anyway, until the awkward silence swallows me. "What happened to the woman who was up there? I figured she'd be riding back with us?"

"Natasha?"

I nod.

"She's agreed to do a few one-on-one meetings with some reporters to go over the firm statement."

I groan.

"What?" His eyes widen right as the elevator door dings.

"Until we have a unified approach, including a narrative we are focusing on pushing, I would strongly prefer no one make any official or unofficial statements."

"You make it sound like a political campaign."

"They're not that different." I follow him into an elevator. "What I'm proposing is a campaign to improve the public perception of your company and its leadership. The thing is, especially in today's climate, you don't want people thinking that your company takes women's rights lightly. And as a car repair company, you want people to trust you."

Ben jabs the button for level two. His teeth are gritted when he says, "I'll call her. Maybe I can prevent a few of the meetings."

Natasha, who is apparently quite dutiful, picks up the second we exit the elevator. He finishes explaining that she should reschedule any meetings and head back right away just as we stop in front of a shiny silver Mercedes.

"Should we wait for her?"

He shakes his head. "She drove separately so she could stick around."

"Got it."

He presses a button and the car chirps. I practically jog to the passenger side and grab the handle, just in case he's thinking of doing something chivalrous or polite and trying to get my door. I cringe at the thought.

It's totally the kind of thing he would have done back in high school.

But when I look his direction, it's clear he knows why I sprinted to the door. His lips curl up, showing just a bit of his beautiful teeth.

I open the door and slide into the pristine car. The seat is beautiful grey leather, but it's not very comfortable. Note to self: when I become a posh person, do not buy a Mercedes. Check out BMW instead. I busy myself with a seatbelt and then whip out my phone to give myself something to do other than stare at him.

Not a single text.

Not even any spam emails.

Not that Ben knows that. I tap away at my screen, as if I have a lot going on. Once he pulls out of the garage and on to the main road, I slide my phone into my purse. "The good news is that the adage, *there's no such thing as bad publicity*, is actually partly true. This media coverage is definitely for a bad reason, but I'm hoping we can turn that attention into something that will be good. In order to do that, we need a compelling strategy."

"Okay."

"I outlined three possibilities before the press conference. One of them is out, since it wasn't you who—" I fake a cough. "But the other two might still work."

"Why did everyone think it was me?" Ben's hands tighten on the steering wheel.

"Your photo was in the paper," I say. "Did you see the article?"

He shakes his head. "It's my photo? Are you sure?"

"Pretty sure. You don't have a very forgettable face."

His head snaps toward me, his eyes scanning me for. . .something. My meaning, maybe?

"You've always been a ridiculously handsome guy," I say. "That can hardly be a shock."

When a smile spreads across his face, it occurs to me that I should *not* be complimenting a married man. What is wrong with me?

"There are really two main ways to handle an affair. The first is an open acknowledgement and penitent apology with promises of better behavior moving forward." I pull some papers out of my briefcase. "This works best when the public really loves someone to begin with. It's essentially the Tiger Woods strategy, though he modified it a bit with the sex-addict line." I pause. "His whole, *It's not my fault!* bit annoyed me, but his devoted fans definitely bought it."

"Okay."

"The other route we can take is to minimize everything as much as possible. Point out any mitigating factors if there are any. Refute erroneous statements, and in my least favorite version, attack the accuser's story." I can't help cringing when I mention this. It's part of the playbook, but I hate it. "This variation *only* works well if the accuser exaggerated some aspect or is lying." I glance sideways to see whether that might be likely.

Ben's knuckles are almost white. I'm guessing that's a no.

"Would your dad be willing to go the penitent route?" My voice is tighter, stiffer than I'd like it to be. "It's the hardest one at the beginning, and it won't work at all if the guilty party is unwilling to publicly apologize."

Muscles in Ben's jaw work. "I'm not sure."

"How did he react when the news broke?"

"I haven't seen him." Ben almost looks frozen in place, eyes ahead, hands at ten and two.

He hasn't seen his dad in the last twenty-four hours? "Maybe it's not true, then," I say. "Maybe it's been exaggerated, or there's another explanation."

"Assume it's all true," Ben says. "I think that's the

most likely scenario, and as much as it pains me to say it, I really doubt dear old pops is going to apologize, to either Mrs. Johnson or to the public at large."

That's a shame.

"Could your mother convince him—"

He shakes his head stiffly.

I drop it. "Alright, well, perhaps when we reach the office, we can go over all the details and facts that you *do* have, and then we can craft an approach specific to this situation."

He turns into a parking lot, slides into a space marked *Vice President* and cuts the engine. "That might be best." He sighs. "Maybe I should have brought that other, overeager PR woman to do all this instead."

His words are like a slap, and heat rises in my cheeks immediately. Is he really that disappointed with my frame up? It's not like I'm working with a lot here. Every idea I've had gets squashed.

When Ben's face turns toward mine and our eyes meet, his widen. "Oh, no. What did I say?"

"That other woman's name is Beatrice Cooper. I can put you in touch, if you'd like." I slide my purse strap over my shoulder. Elana failed to mention that when you have a connection to the person whose account you're trying to acquire, it hurts more if they refuse.

"Addy, why are you upset?"

"I'm sorry for taking up so much of your time." My hand wraps around the handle.

Before I can leave the car, Ben's hand closes over my forearm. "Addy, I meant maybe I should have used her because it's so embarrassing that I know you, and you're learning all these horrible things about my company. About my dad." His voice drops until it's the barest whisper. "About me."

I shift in the seat until I'm facing him directly. "I've

heard nothing bad about you at all. I'm sure your wife has zero complaints."

His face softens. "I'm not married, Addy. We called it off the day before the wedding."

I swallow, trying to buy myself some time. It's not really relevant information to the case at hand, but it still flusters me. Badly. "Right. Okay. Well, that's too bad. But you don't need to worry about what I think. This is my job, and believe me, I've seen worse than this."

"I've imagined bumping into you a lot over the past ten years," he says. "But I never imagined it would be like this."

His words hit me again, but this time it's for a different reason. He's thought about me? *A lot*? I was surprised he even remembered my name after so long, with as fast as he moved on, and with as many girls as he had chasing him.

"Now that I hear those words out loud, they sound a little creepy." Ben winces. "I'm sorry. What I meant to say was that I wish I had seen you again on better terms, but you seem to be very capable, and I'm glad to have someone to help. Clearly this is an 'all hands on deck' situation." He releases me.

I open my door and climb out. I follow him as he walks toward and then inside the building, which is more like an anthill than a corporate office, with people rushing to and fro, all of them waving their hands or carrying papers, all of them in a tizzy, and most of them casting odd looks our way.

"Ben, you're back." A somewhat familiar looking woman with a perfectly coiffed, light brown bob threads her way past the hive of activity to Ben's side in the large open hallway. "How did the press conference go?" The tilt of her head, the press of her lips—I've never seen someone more hopeful.

"We think it would be a good idea to craft a unified message," I say. "My name is Addison Thorley. I'm an account executive at Princeton Public Relations Lab."

The woman breathes a heavy sigh, her eyes still focused on Ben. "It went that badly, huh?"

"It was rough, but Mom, look."

This is his mother? No wonder she seemed like someone I had once met. I try to imagine her with longer hair, pulled back into a ponytail, and I see it.

"Addy really has some great ideas. We need to get together everything you were able to find and have a meeting in the conference room. So far what we've been lacking is any sort of plan."

His mother finally glances my way. "You look—" She blinks, and turns back to Ben. "Why does she look so familiar?"

"We met a long time ago," I say. "When Ben and I were in high school."

Her eyes go as round as saucers. "You're that sweet girl that Benjamin made him dump." She shakes her head. "Well, I won't lie and say I'm happy to see you, not under these circumstances, but I am delighted that someone wants to help us formulate a plan. Clearly we need the help."

❅ 4 ❅

ADDY

TEN YEARS AGO

Sentimentality has ruined my life. I'm the kind of person who's incapable of saying no when it might hurt someone's feelings.

"I can't believe you actually wore those boots." My best friend Mary walks right next to me, her tired, worn sneakers not looking trendy or even especially comfortable.

But at least they aren't three sizes too big and dramatically out of style.

No one will even notice her shoes. They're all too busy gawking at my size ten ski boots from the early nineties. Even though they're in great shape, no one in the world has worn anything with vintage colored rainbow trim in quite some time. Some of the sixth graders streaming past us are even pointing at them. A few are giggling.

"They were the last thing my dad ever gave me," I say. "Otherwise I'd have tossed them years ago. But since I had them, and they're warm, Mom insisted."

Mary's nose scrunches up. Of all the people in all the world, she's about the last one who would ever criticize me. And if her dad ever gave her a gift of any kind, she'd wear it too.

Or maybe she'd burn it.

It's tough to know for sure when something like that has never happened.

"I admire your bold decision, and I'm ready to defend it to the bitter end." She makes her hands into mock guns and shifts round and round, pretending she's ready to fire on the people staring at me.

I may have miserably unfashionable footwear, but not many people have a friend like her. "With two pairs of thick socks on, my feet hardly slide around in them at all, and the weather guy said it's going to snow. When that happens, everyone will be *wishing* they had boots like these."

"You're probably right." She winks.

My mom finishes talking to the camp leader behind us, climbs in her old LeSabre, and waves. She's being uncharacteristically chill—probably because she knows Mary and I are already nervous about being the youngest counselors here and she doesn't want to draw even more attention to us.

Our car backfires twice, but then she backs out of the spot and swings around the corner. I may not have fashionable clothing, and I may be the youngest counselor at camp, but at least I have a loving mother. As Mary's best friend, I've had a front row seat to the evidence that not everyone has that.

Mary shoulders her duffel bag and sighs, just as a shiny black SUV pulls into the parking space my mom just vacated. The sun's shining brightly enough for me to see all seven people in the vehicle, even before they exit.

Mary doesn't wait for the shiny squad to exit—she practically jogs away from them.

I'm happy to head for our cabin, too. My boots make a schlepping, squishing sound with each step. The strange looks and snide comments from both the little kids and the adults when we first arrived are nothing to what the other counselors are going to say, but it's not like the other high school students are our friends. "They weren't going to talk to us anyway."

Mary squares her bony shoulders and smiles. "Who cares? This week is going to be glorious." She inhales deeply. "Mountain air. Crisp weather. Singing birds. Dozens of little kids who listen to our advice and counsel —plus we're missing a week of school."

The red cardinal perched on the pine tree ahead of us really is singing. It's not a melody, *per se*, but he does sound happy. "It's not like we thought being counselors at Camp K.E.E.P. was going to rocket us to instant popularity."

"I didn't think we had a chance of even coming," Mary says. "Much less being counselors alongside six of the most popular kids at school."

"If Hanna and Jane hadn't gotten the flu, we wouldn't be here at all." We've reached our cabin, and a slow, steady chatter of girls' voices behind the door makes me a little bit nervous.

"Push through," Mary says. "We may not have much in common with the other counselors, but the kids will like us just fine."

I hope she's right. I twist the knob and step inside.

Twenty sets of eyes swivel toward the door. They all widen, and then they look us up and down. "I'm Mary," my best friend says. "And I'm a tenth grader at Harcourt High School." She glances my direction, and tosses her head. I wish I had the same confidence and the same commanding air that Mary always has.

"Addison." I swallow. "My name's Addison, but you can call me Addy." And I'm a dope. Pretty much all the time.

"Why did we have to get the counselor with the clown shoes?" The little girl with curly black hair standing near the back of the room folds her arms.

"Maybe that should be our name," the girl next to her says. Her hair's swept into a smooth, high ponytail. "The MoonWalkers."

Everyone giggles.

"Or maybe the Bozos," the girl with dark curls says.

Giggles become guffaws.

Pretty soon everyone is laughing. At me.

So much for the girls idolizing us.

"How about we call ourselves the High Steppers," Mary says. "It means a spirited horse that moves beautifully, or when applied to people, it refers to someone who walks with pride and confidence, just like my friend Addy."

The giggles slowly fizzle out.

"What you may not have realized yet is that it's much harder to wear something practical, or to wear something that people don't know they need yet, than it is to wear something that everyone else has."

"What's she talking about?" The dark-haired girl with curls shrugs and glances around.

"If I walked around the campsite on a bright and sunny day with an umbrella open and ready," Mary says, "I'd look pretty dumb." She pauses until someone else starts to speak. Then she cuts them off, asserting her authority. "Until it started raining. Then I'd be the only person who *didn't* look dumb."

The girls all blink.

"When Bill Gates dropped out of Harvard and

decided to start a computer company, I'm sure a lot of people thought he was being foolish. They might have even laughed. It took a long time for Microsoft to explode, and it took a lot of hard work and insight. No one's laughing at him now. Trust me girls, you want to learn to be like that. Not laughing at the smart people, the people with foresight, that's the first step."

I don't deserve a friend like Mary, truly. She's so smart, so eloquent, and so kind. Her insight has helped me out a million times over the years.

And she's not done yet, apparently. "My friend Addy saw the weather forecast, and she's ready for the snow that's coming. Meanwhile, the rest of us will have cold, miserable feet. So you can mock her right now, or you can be proud, because tomorrow, she's gonna look brilliant."

"My dad did that once," a girl on the very first bed says. She pushes her glasses up her nose. "He put us all in swimsuits on this hike we went on. No one else was wearing them, and they kept itching and they made us all really mad. But then, we reached this waterfall. He'd read the reviews and knew there was one, and we all got to play in it in our suits. When we were done, we weren't stuck hiking back in sopping wet clothes."

"What's your name?" Mary asks.

"Poppy," the girl says.

"Actually, her name is Providence," the girl with dark curls says.

"But I go by Poppy." She pushes her glasses up again. "Like the bright red flower."

I notice that there's a strand of red hair peeking out from under her cap. "I think that's the perfect name for you," I say. "But you shouldn't cover up that gorgeous hair, at least, not until the weather forces you to do it."

We spend the next hour getting to know our twenty girls. At least half of them are terribly obnoxious, but I'm pretty sure that some level of annoyance is a requirement for sixth graders. The other half are adorably eager, hanging on our every word.

"Oh my." Mary glances at her watch. "We'll be late if we don't hurry. We're supposed to be at the cafeteria for lunch in five minutes."

The room dissolves into a flurry of unpacking and shifting and chattering and exclamations. "Does anyone have any dietary restrictions I need to know about?" Mary whips out a checklist, scanning it.

My identical list is in the very bottom of my suitcase. I feel a little guilty that she's stuck with me as her partner. I contribute nothing, and I require epic pep talks just to get the girls to stop laughing at me.

Less than five minutes later, everyone's checked off—no peanut allergies, but one little gal avoids gluten and one is allergic to melon—and we're all ready to go. I step forward to hold the door while the girls filter out and my boots make a squishing sound.

Why, oh why, didn't I insist on bringing some sneakers as well?

"You can borrow a pair of my shoes," the girl with dark curls says. I think she said her name is Chloe. "If we wear the same size." She pauses by the door. "If you want to, just until the snow comes or whatever."

She's nicer than I gave her credit for. "I'm a size eight," I say.

Her nose scrunches. "I'm a size six, so I guess that won't help. Sorry."

I wave her past. "Not unless I wanted to lop off my big toes, and I'm kind of fond of them."

She definitely doesn't get my joke.

Note to self: keep bizarre sense of humor in check. "I was kidding, don't worry." As I follow her out, a brisk wind blows from the top of the mountain toward us.

Mary's at the front like a mother duck, our twenty girls trailing after like dutiful little ducklings. I'm stuck at the back where I belong. I gave Mary that pink scarf for Christmas last year, and with the wind blowing it back behind her, contrasted with her puffy black coat, blonde hair, and her pink cheeks, she looks like a ski club Barbie.

I'm apparently a little too distracted wallowing in my own misfit status to notice other lines of kids, and I'm going just a hair too slow. I nearly crash into one of the other counselors, a big guy named Mike who plays on the football team. I jump out of the way, but my squishy boots don't have the best traction, and when I land on a patch of ice, it's game over. I close my eyes tightly.

My arms pinwheel.

My feet slip up and out.

Just before my head can crack against the pavement, arms reach beneath my armpits and catch me. "Whoa, there."

When I open my eyes, I'm looking at the upside down, but still gorgeous, smiling face of Ben Newberg. Football quarterback. Student Council president.

His arms are still holding me underneath my armpits.

I scramble forward, breaking the contact and freeing myself elegantly—by falling on my backside. "Oof."

"Are you alright?" This time, he's only half-smiling. Concern has begun to replace his good cheer. "I think you hit some ice."

This time the pair of hands that lifts me up, by my upper arms, belong to Mike, the enormous football guy who caused the fall in the first place. "Can't have counselors going down on the first pass."

Pass? What's he talking about?

"I'm Mike," he says.

"An all-around blockhead who clearly doesn't watch where he's going," Ben says.

"Yeah." Mike draws out the word. "Sorry about that." He brushes debris off my sleeves and takes a step back.

There's no sign of Mary or the girls—clearly they didn't see what happened and went right inside. "I'm Addy."

"I'm Ben," Ben Newberg says, as if there's a girl in school who doesn't already know his name.

"Nice to meet you both." I point at the door. "But my friend Mary and all our girls have already gone inside. I better catch up. Thanks for the help." This time, when I dart in front of them, I don't fall. But my boots do make a belching sound as I pass, which sends their boys into fits of laughter.

Great.

By the time I get inside, the last girl in our group is almost done with the food line. It's a cafeteria, so I rush to catch up, cutting in front of another counselor. "Sorry," I say. "I slipped back there, and my girls are just finishing." I snatch a tray and plonk it down on the metal runners.

"You slipped?"

When I look back over my shoulder, Jennifer Young's taking me in with an arched eyebrow. If I thought Mary looked like a Barbie, Jennifer looks like a Ralph Lauren model, from her perfect, fur-topped, black Uggs to her fleecy lavender headband. She's so put together she looks like she came preassembled.

"Uh, yeah. There are ice patches out there."

"Ice patches?" she asks. "Are you sure you didn't trip over your own feet?"

My laugh is nervous—high and shaky. Clearly forced. "Maybe that, too."

"She didn't," Mike says from behind us. "She actually got knocked over, by me. I think her boots are pretty cool. My mom used to have some like that when I was really small."

Words of support and generosity from one of the football players? *That* I did not expect. "You didn't knock me over," I say. "I think it was the other way around. I may just try out for football next year."

Mike's huge laugh floods the cafeteria and reverberates off the walls and ceiling. "You should do that. I'd give you my recommendation for sure."

I turn back to the line, my heart pounding, and scoop things onto my plate at random. I practically scurry to my place at the table, only then realizing that I apparently got a pile of canned peas, a scoop of canned corn, and two chocolate milks. Ugh. While I mix my strange selection around with my spoon, I can't help noticing the other female counselors glancing my way and snickering.

Mary, meanwhile, is telling our girls stories. About me. About herself. About how we met. About the creative things we've made with boxes of macaroni and cheese and things we found in my pantry. They're laughing. They're engaged.

I ignore the rest of the room and focus on our girls. This is why we're here.

After lunch, the faculty from the camp stand up to welcome us all, introduce themselves, and tell us about our goals. "You've been together in middle school for a few months now, and you've probably gotten a pretty good handle on how to succeed academically with multiple teachers, with challenging classes, and with a more rigorous schedule." Mr. Hoover is the name of the Camp Director. He pauses to make sure we're all listening. "But the purpose of our week here is to remind you how to be *friends*. How to have *fun*, even while you're learning. Every year, they threaten to cut our funding. Every year, they put us up for cancellation, and every year

I go and tell them the same thing I'm telling you today. The friendships you have with your fellow students aren't meaningless. They're one of the most important parts of your education. You're learning to work together. You're learning to rely on others. And you're learning to integrate work and play so you can find fulfillment in your work lives for decades to come."

Those are some pretty lofty goals for a sixth grade camp, but he looks like he really means it.

"You're here to work on your environmental and science education this week—almost fifty girls, and forty-nine boys. Take this opportunity to get to know some of your fellow students better, and learn from the counselors who are assigned to stay with you. This afternoon, we're going on a hike—hopefully before the snow blankets the entire area. We've named you after winter birds, so this group—" He points at us. "You're the Cardinals." He points at Mike and Ben's group. "You're the Buntings. You'll be together for this outing, and I'd like you to make sure the boys and girls are mixing."

The murmurs start immediately.

He points at Jennifer and Lacey's group. "Your group of girls will be known as the Robins." He points at the other boys, led by Greg and Scott, basketball players, but also pretty popular. "You're the Woodpeckers."

What was he thinking, using a bird name with 'peckers' in it? I try to ignore the snickering and jokes I hear from half the room.

After we go back to our rooms to grab bags with water, snacks, and extra jackets in case it gets colder, we gather outside, our girls all nervous but excited, and wait to line up for the hike. Mike and Ben and their boys emerge from their tiny bunkhouse moments after we do.

We're lucky enough to have Mr. Hoover leading our hike personally. "Today, we'll be hiking to Valencia Peak.

It's a challenging hike, but I think that together, we'll have a great time. I'm going to be completing the hike with my wife, Laura, and we'll be one crew. Then I'd like each of the counselors to pair up with one guy and one girl. We'll go up the mountain together, but each pair will be assigned to keep track of one-third of the hikers." He walks toward Mary and me and hands us information packets. "Here's the stuff we'll be teaching our little crew in each spot. You should have gotten it by email last week, but I thought a hard copy would be helpful."

Mary beams. "I have another copy I printed at school. It's in my backpack."

"You can take this, then." Hoover offers the packet to Mike.

"Uh, I call being Addy's partner," Mike says. "So maybe give that to him." He tosses his head at Ben.

"Thanks." Ben grabs the packet and raises one skeptical eye at Mary. "I definitely didn't print up my own copy."

The hike is steep, but beautiful. Mike is hilarious the whole way—cracking jokes, teasing the boys and girls alike, and offering bits of information he remembered from the email we got. He backs off and lets me do the teaching every time we stop for specific stuff, but he's ready and happy to chime in and answer questions and explain the complicated parts.

On the way back down, it starts to snow.

At first, it's no big deal. The kids squeal. I hold out my bare palm and watch as snowflakes melt on my skin. By the halfway point, I've zipped my coat up all the way. I've wrapped my scarf around my face. I'm not sharing interesting tidbits anymore.

Chloe, of the dark curly hair, is whining. "I keep slipping."

"My feet are wet," Heather says. "And they're numb."

"Your socks are probably wet." Mike bumps my shoulder with his. "I bet we're all wishing we had some ski boots on right now."

"Yeah, I am." Chloe bobs her head. "Mary was right."

"Mary?" Mike laughs. "Mary's wearing sneakers, too. It's Addy who had the right idea."

Chloe lifts her chin. "But Mary told us we'd regret mocking her."

Mike rolls his eyes. "Should've made my mom get me some."

When we reach camp again, they give us time to change our footwear before dinner, but it doesn't help the people who don't have a second pair, like Mary. I actually feel bad I didn't bring a change of sneakers so she could have them.

When we go to dinner, I pay a lot more attention to the cafeteria food this time. My stomach's completely empty, thanks to my lunch idiocy. "Can I get two rolls?" I ask.

"Two rolls, huh?" Ben's voice behind me is low.

How did I not notice that he was right next to me? "Uh, I didn't eat much for lunch."

"I was just waiting to see if it works to ask for two."

It does.

"I'd like two as well." He shoves his plate out and smiles. He's rewarded with three.

"Growing boys." The cafeteria lady shakes her head, but she's smiling. No one can resist his dimple. It's downright lethal.

Ben follows me to the table, swinging onto the bench next to me and dropping his tray.

"Hey, Ben, over here." Jennifer saved him a spot one table over.

"It's fine," he says.

Greg drops into the seat she saved for him. "Thanks."

Jennifer doesn't look very pleased.

"Hey," Mike says from the back of the line. "What's going on? You trying to steal my hiking buddy?"

"It's the first day," Ben says. "You just met her—I'm not stealing anything." He drops his voice. "But, yes. That's exactly what I'm doing."

My heart hammers in my chest. What's going on? "Mary's a much better partner," I say. "She studied all the materials."

"Oh, I can tell." Ben snorts. "I didn't have to say a word. She knew everything by heart. She's. . .intense."

"Mary's the best."

"You're loyal, too. Color me impressed."

Color him? What's he talking about? "I think the lunch lady has a crush on you."

He sighs. "It's a curse, really. All the wrong ladies like me."

I must be hallucinating, because he glances over at Jennifer. I channel my inner Mary and say what I'm thinking. Boldly. Unafraid. "Really? I think most people would say the head cheerleader and the quarterback are kind of a match made in heaven."

He spears a forkful of green beans. "Hardly."

So I wasn't wrong. "Did you come sit by me to *escape?*"

He glances either direction as if making sure no sixth grade spies are listening. "Escape isn't a strong enough word. For years now, everywhere I go, she's there. It's like she's a hunter and I'm an elk."

"With a huge rack, apparently."

This time, it's Ben's laugh that catches me off guard. "You know, I don't remember ever seeing you before."

"I have a pretty good disguise," I say.

"Oh yeah?" His eyebrows rise. "What is it?"

"I'm a sophomore," I say. "We're basically invisible to seniors."

"Seniors are stupid, because if you'd been a senior, I'd *definitely* have noticed you before now."

Now it's my turn to laugh, only it's the incredulous variety. "You would have—I saw you laughing at my boots."

"It's not he who laughs last that counts," he says. "It's he who laughs longest."

"That phrase doesn't even apply here," I say.

"You're a rough audience." The side of his mouth turns up in a grin. "I like it."

"Nothing about me is easy," I agree.

"I'm learning that," he says. "And I'll admit that I did think your boots looked ridiculous at first, but Mike was right—they're smart."

My revelation for the day is that I'm not as immune to his dimples as I thought I would be.

❧ *5* ❧

BEN

I'm not sure whether it's just bad luck, or whether Fate has a miserable sense of humor. Addy always seems to be around for the low points in my life, when things are all going wrong. Nothing has ever broken the right way with her around.

"I prepared a few scenarios in advance of approaching Ben at the press conference," Addy says, "but it seems that I had a few of the details wrong. I'd love to sit down and develop a timeline so that we can come up with an approach that will work for your company." She's so calm and composed, so professional.

She hasn't even blushed once. It's like the old Addy I knew is gone, replaced by this public relations expert.

I miss the girl who wore enormous boots and a sideways smile.

I miss the girl who looked perpetually unsure but was also eternally optimistic.

I miss the girl who laughed so loud and so long when I made a joke that I felt like I was king of the world.

I hope she's still in there somewhere. If I get half a chance, I mean to find out.

43

"Then by all means." Mom points at the conference room around the corner. "Let's go over all the sordid details."

I suppress a shudder and follow them both into the room with the long wooden table.

Addy whips out a lined pad of yellow paper and circles the table, taking a seat near the end. "I think the best way to start is to tell me the first thing you learned. When did things go wrong?"

"Let's see." Mom takes the seat across from Addy.

I settle next to Mom. It gives me an almost unrestricted view of Addy's face while she fires off questions.

"I'd say the first thing to go wrong was when Benjamin proposed to me. . .and I said yes." Mom's eyebrow quirks. "But I'm guessing you're talking about this particular incident."

Addy's pen freezes an inch above the paper. Her head lifts slowly. "You're saying this wasn't his first. . .indiscretion?"

Mom's laugh is dark. If I didn't know her, I'd probably think it was a little unhinged. "No, it certainly wasn't."

Addy sets her pen down and stares right at Mom. "How many times has he been unfaithful?"

"To the best of my knowledge?"

Addy's sweet face falls. "I'm so sorry." She looks truly pained.

"Don't be sorry—it's not your fault."

"It does mean there's a pattern of misbehavior, and that you all knew about it." The set of her lips is grim.

"This is the first time anyone has alleged that Dad *forced* them to do anything," I say. "Until now, it's always been consensual, as far as we know."

"And to answer the question I think you were asking, we found out about this last night, late. Probably either just before or just after the poor woman contacted the press.”

“It seems like her goal wasn’t to get money,” Addy says. “If she went right to the press.”

“She did ask us for money when she contacted me, but either someone she trusted leaked the information, or she changed her mind and decided to inflict maximum damage instead.”

“It’s possible that if she wins a lawsuit, she’ll manage to do both,” Addy says.

Mom sighs.

The next hour is pretty uncomfortable, as Mom and I detail Dad’s past indiscretions and how they’ve been resolved. Addy tries her best not to look judgmental, I can tell, but it’s hard for her. Finally, after hearing about the eighteen-year-old girl Dad impregnated five years ago, she drops her pen. “I have to ask.” Her voice is sharp, but her eyes are kind. “The most obvious play here is to remove him from leadership, or maybe take the company in a hostile takeover if that’s possible, then distance ourselves from everything to do with him as quickly as possible. Which leads me to the somewhat obvious question of, why haven’t you left him?”

I expect Mom to launch into the speech I’ve heard her make over and over since I was a kid. They’ve been together for decades. Marriage is give and take. No one is perfect. Dad has a lot of good traits, too. I’ve heard it so many times that I could almost recite it myself.

But she doesn’t.

“I’m afraid,” Mom says. “I don’t have a college degree. I have no idea how I’d ever support myself, and I don’t know how it would affect Ben.”

“Ben?” I ask. “As in, me? Your son who’s in his late twenties?”

"There are a lot of reasons." Mom's voice is soft. "You're not the main one, but I do worry."

"Life's too short to spend any of it miserable," Addy says. "Unless one of the reasons is that he makes you happy. . ." Her smile is so forced it pains me.

Mom blinks.

Before she has time to defend Dad again, I blurt out, "Please *never* use me as a reason to stay with him."

Mom stands up abruptly. "I need some air." Her arms and legs move stiffly as she walks out of the room.

"I'm sorry," Addy says. "I think I went too far. Your parents' relationship isn't any of my business."

I'm glad she said it. I've been asking her for years, but it's different coming from an unbiased professional. Which makes me wonder how Addy came back into our lives at all.

"Why did you come to the press conference?" I ask. "When you saw me in the paper, I'd have thought you'd count yourself lucky to have avoided all this." She thought it was *me* who had pressured that poor woman.

Addy's face falls. "Not everything is about you, you know. I'm a hard worker, and I'm good at what I do. I'm up for a promotion that I deserve—but I won't get it unless I start bringing in new clients. It was dumb luck that today's paper had your face on the front, and I couldn't quite pass up the chance to land a new client. Now that I'm here, I really do want to help, and not only because it's my job."

I should have known it was something like that. "Let's see what we can come up with."

If I thought she'd changed from the wide-eyed optimist I knew before, the next two hours only confirms it. She may no longer be a blind optimist, but Addy's bright, competent, and clever. She reviews details for another half an hour or so, and then starts sketching out options. This is the first time we've had to deal with one of Dad's affairs publicly, and I'm sick about the fact that he appears to have pressured an employee, but in some ways, it's almost nice that other people know the truth.

"Our best bet, then," Addy says, "is to go with that second option. I'll head back to the office and go over the details with my boss, and once I have his input I'll put together press releases and—"

The door to the conference room opens so hard it slams back against the doorstop on the wall.

Mom's standing in the doorway, her cream wool jacket over her arm, her eyes a little wild. Her mascara's smudged under her left eye, like she's been crying. That's hardly a shock, given the day we've had.

"Are you alright?" I ask.

"We have a plan that we'd be happy to review with you," Addy says. "Would you like to sit down?"

Good thinking. Mom looks like she needs a little timeout.

"Your dad and uncle started this business before we met," Mom says. "If he had started it after we married—but he didn't." Her lips twist. "I called a lawyer today and asked him about it. I sent him the files from the incorporation."

"Wait, Uncle Chris?" I frown. "I didn't know—"

"He was a silent investor—he provided the money, and your dad did everything else. He's a passive partner, but he owns forty percent."

That's a surprise. Dad never mentioned his involvement, and other than holidays, we never see him. I've never even heard him ask about our business.

"The reason I looked it up. . ." Mom twists her hands around and round, her coat sliding off her arm and falling to the floor. She looks up at me, her eyes wide and almost *frightened.* "Something about hearing the words out loud —I know it's not a good time. I know that, especially after all this time, leaving your father. . ." She clears her throat. "But I did it. That lawyer I spoke with is going to serve divorce papers on your father tomorrow."

"Why would now be a bad time?" I ask. "If I knew you wanted to leave him, I'd have been supportive twenty years ago." Well, maybe not twenty. I could barely tie my own shoes. But it conveys my point.

"Addy said our best play would be to kick him out," Mom says. "And since I don't own any part of the company, and you only own a fractional share your dad has been passing through the family trust to you as a passive partner—"

If she leaves him, there's no way he'll agree to distance himself from the company. "But even if you stayed with him, we couldn't kick him out," I say. "It's not like your divorce changes that. In fact, by the time it's done, maybe we *will* be able to. Who knows?"

"Ben owns a fractional share?" Addy asks. "Like what kind of share?"

Mom bites her lip.

"I'm not sure," I say. "When I was ten, a lawyer advised Dad to start moving a portion of the business every year, so that there wouldn't be huge estate taxes when he died."

"I think it's around fifteen or twenty percent," Mom says. "I can find the statement from last year. But it's very specific that he's a passive owner and has no control rights."

"But if your uncle agreed with you," Addy says, "then maybe you *could* remove your dad from leadership."

Forty percent plus fifteen or twenty is more than fifty. Why didn't I think of that?

"Uncle Chris and your dad are still close," Mom says. "He'd never agree."

"And until five minutes ago," I say, "I'd have said that my mother would never even *consider* leaving my father." I shrug. "It's rare, but sometimes things change."

"Let's call your uncle," Mom says. "I heard Addy's leaving, but I'd love it if she could be present when we meet with him."

Even Mom recognizes what an asset Addy has been. I look up Uncle Chris' number on my phone and dial it on the bizarrely shaped company speakerphone that sits in the center of the conference room table.

"Hello?" Uncle Chris' voice is perpetually rough, like he was up all night at a smoky club or something.

"Uncle Chris?"

"My favorite nephew!"

"I'm your only nephew," I say.

"You're still my favorite," he says. "Good to hear from you."

"Unfortunately, we're not calling with great news." Mom drops a hand onto my shoulder. "I hate to do this Chris, but we need to meet with you. It's about the company—and about Benjamin."

His voice is flat. "I saw the news."

"You can probably guess what we need to talk about, then," Mom says.

"I suppose it can't be helped," he says.

For some reason, the droll way in which he accepts that we need to talk gives me hope. I know he loves Dad —they were always close. He even gave him the capital to start this business. But surely even Uncle Chris will see what we already know.

Dad has got to go.

Afterward, Addy stands up, takes the plan she made and wads it into a ball. She tosses it into the trashcan—

making the shot. "Looks like we need a new plan," she says. "And I have to say, I'm delighted to hear it."

She's as fabulous as she ever was.

But I still miss the boots.

50

❧ 6 ❧

BEN

****TEN YEARS AGO****

I'm terrible at the guitar.

It never really bothered me before.

Mom made me take piano lessons for two years before I convinced her that guitar would be an adequate substitute. My semi-formed dreams of becoming a lead singer in a band fueled the switch, but I wasn't any better at guitar than I was at the piano. Practicing guitar was still a drag, and I avoided it whenever possible.

It never really bothered me that I wasn't particularly musically inclined.

Until now.

Mike's playing *"Everything You Want"* by Vertical Horizon, and Addy's singing along—with her friend Mary and Lacey, since Jennifer can't sing at all—and my fist is aching to punch him in the nose. Which is crazy. Everyone loves Mike. He's my best friend.

I just wish Addy was looking at me like she's looking at him, all warm and bright and cheerful. When he finally stops, I hold out my hand.

"Whoa," Mike says. "You want to play?"

I roll my eyes. "Please. I play guitar all the time."

"If by *all the time*, you mean once a week at your lessons, then sure."

"You take guitar lessons?" Addy's eyes are ridiculously hopeful. It makes me twice as nervous.

"He introduced me to my teacher," Mike says with a mischievous look in his eye. "He's been playing for *years* longer than me."

"Years longer?" Addy's eyebrows rise. "Wow, you must be really great."

Now there's no way I'm going to play.

"He is good," Jennifer says. "I have a recording he made me."

Addy's head whips around so fast, it makes me dizzy. "He recorded songs for you? Which ones?"

"I had to record them for my teacher," I explain. "Jennifer swiped it after he gave it back."

Jennifer's beautiful, but not when she's pouting. Lately, it feels like she's always pouting.

"I can't play at all," Addy says.

"Me either," Mary says.

That makes me feel a little better. If they don't play, maybe they won't notice when my fingers aren't quite right or when I drop notes. I want to play something soulful, something they can sing to, but I haven't really learned any of those kinds of songs.

"What about '*Hotel California*'?" Mike says. "That's a good one that people know."

"Not me, unfortunately." I check the tuning to have something to do. "I could do—"

"What about '*Free Fallin'*'?" Mary asks. "By Tom Petty?"

"'*Free Fallin'*'?"

"It's Addy's favorite song," Mary says. "We had to

listen to it on repeat the summer she discovered Tom Petty." Mary smirks at her friend.

"I know that one." Mike snatches the guitar back and is playing before I have time to object. As Mary said, Addy knows every word.

"That was amazing," Addy says. "It's so cool you can just play songs like that. Without music, without anything."

"It's really just basic chords," Mike says. "I think it's cooler that you can remember all the words."

"Obsessive." Mary coughs.

For sophomores, they're both pretty funny.

"Well, I'm very impressed," Addy says.

A pulse of jealousy shoots through me. I know exactly one great song on the guitar, and even if it's not one that anyone is going to sing along with, I'm going to play it if it kills me. I pluck the guitar off the table and start to play '*The Devil Went Down to Georgia.*'

I don't even dare to look at Addy during the song or Mary either. That leaves me looking at Jennifer, but that's okay. It's not like it was romantic. But when I finish, it's not Addy or even Mary who's exclaiming.

"I wish I'd recorded that," Jennifer says. "I'd listen to it every day."

"What a showoff." Mike's smiling his signature, goofy grin.

Addy stands up, her big boots squeaking against the tile floor.

"You headed to bed already?" Mike asks.

We get exactly one hour after the kids go to bed to hang out, and the clock shows that we're down to ten minutes left. It's stupid, but I don't want to waste the last ten minutes.

And I'm sick of sharing.

"I wanted to go for a walk." I stand up, too. "Feel like getting one last burst of exercise before you go to sleep?"

"I'll go," Jennifer says. Somehow, in a split second, she manages to stand up and slide her arm inside of mine. I swear, she's like a human barnacle.

"You were just saying that your shoes and socks were wet all the way through and you couldn't wait to go change into pajamas," Mike says. "As your friend, I can't in good conscience allow you to risk yourself like that."

When I meet his eye, he winks at me. And that's why I love Mike. He can clearly tell that I like Addy, and he's blocking Jennifer from her ridiculous *mine mine mine* act.

"But I think—"

Before she can argue more, Mike throws his arm around her shoulders and pries her away from my side.

"I'm cold too." Mary yawns. "I better head right back to the cabin."

"But no one has even heard me play," Greg says. "I know how to play '*Hotel California.*'"

"I'd love to hear it," Lacey says.

"Me too," Scott says. "My dad loves that song."

They're laughing as I walk Addy out. After Mary peels off toward her cabin, and Mike practically shoves Jennifer down the path toward hers, it's just the two of us.

"Aren't you cold?" Addy looks at my sneakers. "Aren't *your* socks wet?"

"We can't all be brilliant and perfectly equipped," I say. "But so far I'm fine." That's a lie. My feet are absolutely freezing, but some things matter more than toes.

Before I can even think about reaching for her hand, she tugs her hat down further on her head and stuffs both hands into her puffy coat pockets.

"Where did you want to go?"

I point. "Not far. We only have ten minutes." Or like, eight now. "Maybe to the top of that bluff."

She shrugs. "Alright."

"Why did you get those boots, anyway?" I ask. "Do you do a lot of skiing?"

She laughs. "I've never been skiing *or* sledding either. But my dad is one of those guys who love to dream big. He's always starting new businesses, even though they inevitably bust."

"Bust?"

She turns her head sideways and meets my eye. That's when I notice she has the cutest little freckle right by the corner of her left eye. I want to reach out and touch it. I'm dying to know whether it's flat, or whether I could feel its shape.

"They fail," she says. "My dad used to run a Payless Shoe Store—but managing one of those didn't pay very well, as you might imagine."

"What does that have to do with ski boots? Did they sell those at Payless?"

She blushes, and it's the cutest thing I've ever seen. "No. But Dad decided that we didn't have any ski shops in Atlanta, and—"

"What about Rocky Mountain Board—"

"This was a while ago. It wasn't around yet."

"Okay."

"He met this guy who was in charge of purchasing for a ski shop in Vail." She sighs. "Or at least, that's what he said. He told my dad he could buy all their surplus for super cheap."

"Oh."

She stops walking and looks down at her boots. "My dad was a sucker—we got stuck with a ton of really old surplus gear."

Geez.

"And Dad emptied his retirement fund to buy it."

"He didn't."

She sighs again. "We ended up having to sell it online and at garage sales any way we could. Now we still have boxes of old weird sizes like this in the garage, and when Mom found out this was in the mountains. . ."

"They may be too big for you, but they do look warm." Plus, they're the reason I noticed her in the first place. Maybe I owe her dad a big *thank you.* The more time I spend talking to Addy, the more I like her.

"What about you?" she asks. "What does your dad do?"

"He runs an automotive repair chain," I say. "So if you ever need your brakes fixed." I chuckle.

"Are you good at fixing cars?"

I shake my head. "Not at all. I don't know the slightest thing about it, and neither does my dad. He had a professor in business school tell him that it wasn't really about finding something you wanted to sell. Success came from finding an underserved area in the market. When we moved to Atlanta, our car broke down and Dad had to wait for two days to find a place with the space to fix it. A few days of research later, he discovered that Atlanta had thirty percent fewer auto repair shops than any other city of its size on this side of the country. He got funding for his first shop that next week."

"He sounds smart." She looks glum, for some reason.

Oh, right. Her dad keeps having ideas, but none of them work. *Change the subject, idiot.*

"How did you get chosen as a counselor, since you're a sophomore?"

She smirks. "That's all Mary. She insisted that we apply, saying that if we got lucky, we'd miss a week of school."

"And it worked."

"It wouldn't have, except those other girls got sick." She shrugs.

"I'm glad they did," I say. "I'd probably never have met you, otherwise."

"Yeah, I'm a real catch." She's staring down at her boots.

I lift her chin until she's looking at me. "I think you are."

Her eyes widen. Her breathing speeds up.

"Now, I have a question to ask you." I step a bit closer.

She nods.

I drop my hand and smile. If I've learned anything so far, it's that the longer you can make someone wait for something, the better it is. "Tomorrow, when we go on our next hike. . ."

"No," she says.

"No?" My eyebrows shoot up. "I haven't even asked anything yet."

Her hand comes out of her pocket and rests on her cocked hip. "They might be big enough, but you cannot borrow my boots, Mr. Newberg, no matter how cute your dimples are."

She thinks my dimples are cute? "I wasn't trying to—"

Addy rolls her eyes. "Duh. I'm kidding. What did you really want?"

I splutter. "Tomorrow, don't go with Mike."

"Mike?"

"I don't mind you being his friend—everyone loves Mike—but I want to be your hiking partner tomorrow. How else am I going to find the time to flirt with you as much as I want?"

This time, I can see her blush even in the near dark. "The thing is, Ben—"

I like the sound of my name when she says it. "No, there's no thing. Just say okay. You'll be my hiking partner."

She purses her lips, but then she nods. And my heart

soars. I walk her back then—I don't want to get yelled at on our first day for breaking rules.

Only, the next day, Mike and I are assigned to go out with Jennifer and Lacey. I beg and I complain and I cajole, and it doesn't matter. Hoover insists. "You'll be partnered with the Cardinals again tomorrow," he says. "But right now, you're with the Robins."

Which means the only time I even see Addy all day is at meals, and with the disconnect between when we get to the cafeteria and when their group does, I don't even get to sit by her.

Possibly because I've shown an interest in her, Greg and Scott are on her like white on rice. Hearing her laugh in response to things Scott's saying makes me ball up my napkin. I want to smash my cup and throw it at their heads. Or something worse. But I don't. I'm perfectly behaved.

I do catch her looking at me a few times.

After dinner, Hoover leaves us his guitar to play with again, only this time, I'm ready. I practiced this morning before anyone else was up, and thanks to the magic of the Internet and pirated sheet music, I can play '*One Last Breath*' by Creed reasonably well. I flub it in a few places, but when I finish, I make sure to look right at Addy, not at Jennifer.

"That was really good," Addy says.

"Imagine how good he could be if he actually practiced," Mike says. "His mother will be delighted."

"About what?" I ask.

"If she had known all it took was a cute sophomore to get you to practice, she'd have been shoving them at you years ago." Mike's smirking.

I am so going to punch him later.

But Addy's blushing brightly, and my anger evaporates. So what if she knows I want to impress her? It's true.

"You should come see him play football," Mike says. "He's way better at that than he is with a guitar."

I shove him.

Jennifer stands up. "I was thinking maybe I'd take a walk."

Addy looks down at her hands.

"You should," I say. "Hey Greg, why don't you go with her?"

He hops to his feet quickly, and before Jennifer can argue, he and Scott walk her out the door. I wait for the next forty minutes, hoping Addy will want to go for a walk, or pay any attention to me at all, but she never budges.

I don't leave either.

Eventually, Mike and I play her and Mary a game of team spades—they're basically impossible to defeat.

"No way," Mike says. "How could you possibly go blind low again? Eventually, you're going to get the ace of spades, and then where will you be?"

Addy shrugs. "Hasn't happened yet."

"You two must play this a lot," I say.

"The summers go by faster with a friend," Mary says. "And my little sister Trudy's a good sport about losing."

The next few days fly by too fast. I manage to beat Mike out and hike with her on not one, but two different trails, but before I know it, it's Friday afternoon. That means it's time to go home.

The boys are frantically stuffing their messes into their bags, and I've never seen so many dirty socks in my life.

"Hey, are you packed?" Mike asks.

I lift my bag by way of response.

"It was a pretty fun week," Mike says. "Or at least, I had a great time."

I bob my head. "More fun than when we came as kids, even."

"Some of that probably has to do with Addy." Mike's grin is a little smug, but he's been cool so I don't get annoyed.

"Maybe it does." I shrug.

Mike sits down on the edge of my now stripped mattress. "Here's the thing. I know you like her. I like her, too."

"Whoa." My heart picks up. "You *like* her?"

Mike laughs. "You are super dense when you're into someone. No. I like her, like if she was my little sister."

"She's not that much younger than we are," I say.

"Oh my gosh." Mike exhales. "You're like a dog that's so focused on chasing the squirrel that you're totally missing the point."

"What's the point?"

"You're like a god back at school. It's been nice to have this little break from reality, but you and I both know what will happen next week."

I can't help my frown. "What does that mean?"

"Jennifer has been a constant in your life," Mike says. "You're interested in a new girl every week, but you always come back to Jennifer, and she never gives up on you." He shakes his head. "It's messed up, but I don't usually care."

But he likes Addy. That's why he started with that.

"I'm not some kind of scoundrel," I say. "It's not like I'm sleeping with anyone."

Mike snorts. "Alright—you're an all-around saint. I'm just saying." He stands up, squaring his shoulders and flexing. I've never paid much attention to Mike being a few inches taller than me, but then he's never *loomed* quite like this. "*Be* a saint with her. Either lose interest quickly, or don't lose interest at all."

"You're acting like you're her dad or something," I say. "I already told you—I'm not a villain."

"Then don't act like one, and we'll be cool." Mike grabs his bag off the floor and marches out the door, not even paying attention to whether any of the boys follow him.

He says he doesn't like her, but it makes me wonder. Mike has never cared what I did with any girl before—he doesn't really date much himself. He's just friends with everyone. Does he like her, and he's warning me off? Or is it really what he says? Is he worried I'll hurt her feelings, and he doesn't want that?

Either way, it doesn't matter. I really do like Addy, and it doesn't feel like anything else I've felt. In the past week, I've liked her more every day. Once the last of the boys are packed and the room's clear, I duck outside.

Jennifer's mom is waiting for us in her huge SUV, but I'm surprised to see Mary and Addy waiting in line for the bus with the little kids. I jog over to where Addy's standing near the front of the line. "Whatcha doing?"

"My mom has to work," she says. "She's going to pick us up from the school later."

Jennifer and Mike are waving at me, and Mike shouts. "Let's go!"

I think about Monday morning—what it'll be like. All my friends, Mike, Jennifer, Greg, Scott, Lacey, all the others. Mike's right—it'll be different, no matter how easy it's been here. Addy's a sophomore. She doesn't know any of them. They won't understand why we're friends, and if I'm not careful, I'll end up hurting her without meaning to.

Which means I'll need to be really careful.

I throw my hand out and wave Mike and Jennifer back. "I'll text my mom. I'm taking the bus."

Mary's eyes fly wide, and Addy's jaw actually drops. "You're what?"

"My mom might even drop off my car. I could give you two a ride home if she does."

Addy swallows, but she doesn't answer.

"I told you he liked you," Mary says. "Hey. Wait up!" She jogs up the steps and slides into a seat with the redhead she's always talking to from their group.

"Looks like you and I could share a seat," I say. "I promise not to bite."

Addy laughs.

I love the sound. "Is that a yes?"

She bobs her head. I have no idea why she's so much shyer right now than before—maybe this is how Cinderella felt on her way home from the ball. Like the magic was drifting away and she ought to hide. Unlike that idiot prince, I'm following her pumpkin coach home so I don't lose her.

Even if the coach is a big yellow school bus.

I make dumb jokes and ask her more about her family, and then we talk about music, and before I know it, I'm almost out of time again. I pull out my phone. My mom texted back.

HAVE A MEETING, BUT I HAD DWIGHT LEAVE YOUR CAR. KEY'S UNDER THE GAS COVER. SEE YOU SOON.

My mom's the best. Like, really the best.

"Turns out, I can give you both a ride." It occurs to me that her mom might already be there, waiting. "Unless your mom's waiting on you."

"She was going to be half an hour late," Addy says. "I'll text her and let her know."

I can't help my smile. Once she's done texting, I snatch her phone and save my number in it. "Now you can text me, and then I'll have your number too." I hold her phone out to her. When our hands brush, I realize this is the first time we've touched without gloves on. It's been a cold week—but the chill that runs up my arm this time has nothing to do with the temperature.

"Thanks," she says.

"You haven't texted me yet."

She laughs. "Fine."

When my phone chimes, I check to see what she said.

BOO.

HAPPY HALLOWEEN. I text back.

TRICK OR TREAT, she texts me. When I look up at her, she's smiling and biting her lip at the same time. My eyes get stuck looking at her lips. They're delicate, makeup free, and shiny. Her teeth aren't perfect, but I love how the left one crosses over the right one just a bit. It gives her character.

I ALWAYS CHOOSE TREATS.

She rummages around in her bag and pulls out a Jolly Rancher.

"That's not the kind of treat I had in mind," I say.

"Oh?"

We're pulling into the parking lot, and her friend Mary's about to rejoin us. "I was thinking you might let me buy you dinner."

She freezes, like I suggested we strip down naked. Or knock over a bank.

"Uh-oh, what did I do? Do you not eat dinner?"

Her laugh's forced. "I do eat dinner, but my mom has this rule."

"A rule that keeps you from eating?"

"Of course not," she says.

"Then do it with me. Tonight, even."

"I can't date," she says. "Not until I turn seventeen."

"Oh," I say. "Wait, how old are you?"

"I turn sixteen in ten days."

I don't swear. I don't even scowl. "Wow, I did not realize you were that young."

"Sophomore." She shrugs. "I didn't hide it."

No, she didn't. Ugh. "Maybe she'd change the rule to sixteen?" I hate how hopeful I sound. "Parents like me. I could talk to them."

She laughs. "She probably would like you, but meeting you would only make her more positive. Trust me on that."

"That sucks," I say. It really, really, sucks. In fact, I'm so bummed that I can't even put it into words. Which is stupid. I barely know her, but I want to know her better. I want a lot more than a week. I want dinners. And I want to take her to see movies. And I want to, I don't know, go on a picnic, or whatever stupid stuff people do when they have a girlfriend.

I want Addy to be my girlfriend.

I don't want anyone else to ask her out or hold her hand.

Without thinking, without pondering, I slide my hand over hers and press my fingers between her tiny ones. "It really sucks."

"It does." Addy squeezes my hand.

And my heart flips in my chest.

I'm almost eighteen years old, and my heart has never done that in my entire life.

I want to feel it again—badly. I want to keep Addy by my side. I want to argue with her parents until they agree that we can spend time together. I want to—

"Mom lets me go to school dances."

What? What's she saying?

"Like, for instance, I went to Homecoming with Paul Brighton."

Who the heck is Paul Brighton? I have a pulsing desire to hit him in the face.

"With prom coming up. . ."

"Oh." Oh! "You're saying I could take you to prom."

"Mom allows it, if it's a double date. So if another couple comes along, then I can go," she says. "I mean, if you wanted to take me."

"I do." I don't hesitate. "I want to take you to prom, and I'm sure Mike will support the cause and come with us."

Addy's beaming, and it's even better than when she laughs. "Alright."

"Alright." This time, *I* squeeze *her* hand.

And even so, my heart flips again.

"When you meet with them later today, we'll need them to sign this retainer agreement," Harriet says, "but it sounds like that's a mere formality at this point. Nice work! They're a huge company, and this is a big deal."

"You've got this in the bag." Elana looks smug, as if she's the one up for a promotion.

"Not quite," Harriet says. "The thing is, you're a harder worker, and your ideas are better, but one client isn't a silver bullet."

She's right, of course. "Do you have any other suggestions?"

Harriet's the best—she spends the next twenty minutes giving me ideas. "One of the most important things we do as PR people is to be prepared for whatever comes so we always look around the bend. For instance, make sure that you've got a plan, no matter which way things go with the uncle. You can't forget, no matter how you feel about Ben and his mother, that the client is the company, and right now, that's led by the philanderer."

I forget what I was about to say. "What?"

"You can't put all your hopes on the son and the mother wresting control from the dad."

"That's the best message for Newberg Automotive Repair," I say. "That they really are focused on honesty."

Harriet stands up. "You're unbelievably naive." She brushes invisible lint off her pants. "We're a PR firm. It's literally our job to repair the bad things our clients do. We bill for our time, except in the rare instance where we have a fixed project fee. It's actually in our best interest if they can't oust the perv." The set of her lips is bemused.

"But we want justice for that woman and the best future for our client."

"We didn't create this situation," she says, "and we want to turn it around, but just consider how much more impressive it would be for you if you bring in a client who needs months and months of our help, instead of a few press releases and a rug sweep."

I can hardly believe what she's saying.

"In any case, the notion of this uncle turning on his own brother is a long shot. Before you leave, I expect a full proposal for how you'll pivot when that fails."

"I can't bill them—"

"You won't be able to bill anyone if you don't snag the client and keep them. Do as I said." She's shaking her head as she walks away.

I really hope she's not right, but I do as she orders, fleshing out the details of the original plan Ben and I worked up, before his mother announced her intention to divorce his philandering father. I barely get her approval before it's time for me to rush out to meet Ben and his mother.

Ben's mother looked fairly put together yesterday in her sweater set and conservative skirt, but today she looks ready to go to war. Her business suit is black with white piping, and her heels are high. Her hair is perfectly done, and her makeup is flawless.

Her son was probably born ready. His golden hair shines. His suit is pristine. His smile is wry.

But why do they look like this for a meeting with Ben's uncle? Shouldn't they be less formal when asking a family member a favor?

I suppose asking him to turn on his own brother is a bit more than a favor.

Maybe they are going to war.

"Where are we meeting him?" I ask.

"I suggested Pricci," Ben says. "There isn't a better Italian place in Atlanta, and Uncle Chris loves ravioli."

"You did?" Ben's mom asks. "I texted to recommend Pasta da Pulcinella." She sighs.

A tall man with broad shoulders and the exact same eyes as Ben walks through the door, dressed in a beautiful charcoal grey suit. "I told you both that you didn't need to buy me a meal. I'm overdue to check out the corporate headquarters anyway. And if we're going to talk business, we may as well do it here. At the scene of the so-called crime."

So-called? Is there a chance Benjamin Newberg didn't do what the woman said? Ben and his mother didn't even mention that as a possibility. I open my mouth to ask.

"Shall we?" Uncle Chris runs a hand through his greying hair and points at the conference room.

Ben's brow is furrowed and his hands are clenched into fists. Maybe it's not the best time for me to get into that question. Ben and his mother walk through the door, and I follow. Ben circles the table and his mother follows. They both sit next to one another on the far end.

Uncle Chris sits directly opposite Ben.

I'm not sure where I should sit. If I sit by Ben's mother, it looks like we're ganging up on him, three to one. If I sit on the end, it's like I'm declaring myself the boss. But I can't sit by Uncle Chris, since he doesn't know me.

After a moment of indecision, all three of them look up at me and I panic and pull out the chair on the end of the table. Hopefully they won't read much into it.

"Who is she?" Uncle Chris asks.

"She's our public relations account executive," Ben's mother says. "She's an old friend of Ben's from high school, and she showed up at precisely the right time. We had no idea what to do. We're in quite a mess, you know, a mess your brother caused, again."

Uncle Chris grimaces.

"We haven't bothered you with most of it," Ben's mother says. "We've tried to keep everything as quiet as possible, but last night, I put together a timeline. It includes all the affairs I know about, but I'm guessing it's not all of them. Just the ones where he's been caught." She places a piece of paper on the table.

"Did you put this together just for me?" Uncle Chris raises his eyebrows. "Or was this for your *divorce lawyer?*"

She folds her arms. "I'm not going to apologize. I did it for you *and* for the lawyer. Chris, you love your brother and that's admirable. You've always supported him, but he's just like your father was. I should have done this years ago." She glances at me furtively, as if she has me to thank for her new resolve.

Uncle Chris leans toward her, his hand flat on the heavy wooden table. "Viv, you've been together for more than thirty years. Divorcing him isn't something you should do lightly."

She shoves the paper at him and it bunches up against his thick fingers. "Lightly?" Her voice is high and shrill. "There are almost twenty affairs on this paper, Chris. *Twenty.* That I know about. Your brother has been more than unfaithful. He's been *awful.* I'm ashamed that I didn't leave him twenty-eight years ago." She inhales deeply and leans back in her seat, folding her hands in front of her. "But this meeting isn't about my divorce. It's not even about taking away your brother's property. The divorce may or may not grant me partial ownership in this business—that's for a judge to decide."

"What do you want, then?" Uncle Chris asks.

"He needs to be removed from leadership," Ben says. "Surely you can see that this isn't like the other affairs. As far as we know, it's the first time Dad has forced himself on someone. He assaulted an *employee.*" Ben shakes his head. "There may be criminal charges."

"She *says* he did. Instead of supporting your dad, you're just accepting it?" Uncle Chris looks scared, but he sounds angry. "Is that what family means to you?"

"Family takes care of you," Ben says. "Family serves you. Family lifts you up."

"Your dad paid for your fancy college degree," Uncle Chris says. "He bought you cars. He bought you clothes. He bought you—"

"Yes, he bought me a lot of things," Ben says. "I've never denied that—but family's more than money. What has he *taught me?* He's taught me to put money first and relationships last. Well, guess what? Right now, putting money first means eliminating the liability he presents to this company. To keep his company viable, we need to eliminate his control over it and his stain upon it. I'm asking you, as an investor, to vote that he be removed from leadership. Then we can proceed by telling the press what we've done and taking responsibility for better management in the future."

"Have you talked to him?" Uncle Chris asks. "What does he say about it? Does he admit that he accosted her?"

Ben's hands grasp the edge of the table tightly. "He says he's innocent of that—he says their relationship was consensual."

"Don't you think that nineteen other affairs in which no one ever alleged this sort of thing are evidence that he *isn't* the kind of person to force anyone?" Uncle Chris looks almost. . .proud. . .of his brother.

It gives me the willies.

He turns toward me. "You're a public relations expert. Isn't it your job to help clean up the firm's image no matter what we do? No matter what the facts?"

"Well, I—er, I mean, yes. It's our job to help companies present their best image no matter what the situation."

"If I decide to support the hard-working, brilliant CEO who expanded this company a hundredfold instead of turning on him, you can help us clean up the corporate image, right?"

I swallow. "It will be quite difficult to clean up the company's image if their active CEO is arrested for sexual assault."

Ben slams his hand on the table. "How can you support him when he's *still* ruining everything?"

Uncle Chris stands up. "I'm ashamed of you. My brother may have made a mistake—I imagine we've all made plenty. But you're listening to the words of that woman instead of him. You're ready to forget about all the good things he's done, how he went to every single one of your track meets and football games, Ben, how he proudly attended your graduation after paying for your tuition, your board, your tutors, everything. How he brought you into his business and then started transferring shares to you immediately in that family trust." He shakes his head. "All of that's worth, what? Nothing?"

He spins on his heel and heads for the door, but he

pauses before opening it. "And you." He stares pointedly at me and purses his lips. "If I hear that you're pushing this agenda of trying to oust my brother, I'll have you fired quicker than you can say 'affair.' If you work for this company, you work *for* my brother, not against him."

ADDY

"That was disappointing," Ben's mother says, "but not totally unexpected."

Ben looks like someone socked him on the jaw. "It was to me."

"You thought Chris would come in on his white horse and save us?" Her laugh is part bitter, part despairing. "Real life doesn't boast many white knights, I'm afraid."

She's not wrong about that. "We have to clean up the mess ourselves." Women have learned that the hard way over the past few centuries. Maybe the past few millennia.

"I'm sorry," Ben says. "I shouldn't have gotten everyone's hopes up." He pats the table. "Maybe we can put together the basics of that plan we were working on yesterday."

I hope he's not mad that my boss already had me put it together. "Actually—"

"I know I chucked it in the trashcan yesterday, but if Uncle Chris isn't on board, there's not much we can do."

"If I had started this process earlier," Ben's mother says, "maybe we'd have more options."

"Recriminations and what-ifs don't help," I say. "Trust me, I know. And this morning, my boss made me prepare a contingency plan, in case this meeting didn't go well."

"See, Mom?" Ben shakes his head. "I told you she's brilliant."

Her shoulders slump. "Yes, you did." When she stands up, it reminds me of a marionette, her arms and legs moving listlessly, as if someone else is forcing her.

"It'll be okay," I say. "You're still going to get free. Once the divorce is finalized, however it shakes out, you can either distance yourself from the drama, or kick him out then."

Her laugh's hollow. "Right, that's true. I just need to keep the company in one piece until then, right?" Her forced smile doesn't reach her eyes.

"My uncle refused to eat lunch, but I'm starving," Ben says. "Would you want to go over the plan while we eat, by chance?"

Is he asking me on a date? Or is this simply an expedient time to talk?

Don't be stupid, Addy. It's clearly a working lunch.

"Sure," I say. "I could eat."

"How do you feel about Korean?"

"I'm not sure I've ever had it." I bite my lip.

"There's a great deli I love around the corner—Kwan's. It has sandwiches and whatnot, if you don't want to get any more adventurous."

"That's fine." If he loves it, it's the best place we can go. After the last few days, I'm sure he needs some familiar food he enjoys.

"You really ought to try the bulgogi," he says. "It's so good. If you're not really big on meat, you can get bibimbap, which is where they toss in vegetables too."

"Bimbap?" I laugh. "That's a funny name, but I do love vegetables. Maybe I'll try that."

He spends most of the short walk over telling me about how he first tried it by accident. "A delivery guy showed up and dropped off an order for Ben—I had ordered sandwiches—but it was bulgogi instead. They told me to wait and they'd bring my order, but by the time they did. . .I'd already eaten the other guy's food."

His chagrined smile is about the cutest thing I've ever seen.

I need to get my feelings under control, because the last time I felt like this, things did not end well for me.

But I haven't liked anyone this much since. . .since the last time I liked Ben. Ugh. How depressing. "Maybe the smell will win me over, too."

We've reached his little deli, and it's cute. A maroon awning covers tables and chairs on the outside, but there's seating inside as well. The staff all smile as we walk inside. And the smell of barbecue and savory seasonings floods my nostrils. He was right—I'm already salivating.

"I think that bimbap stuff sounds good," I say. "I'm kind of excited to try it."

"You won't be disappointed," he says. "But it's actually *bi*bimbap. I think the 'bibim' part means mixed veggies or something, and the bap means rice."

"Alright, I'll give it a shot."

"Mr. Ben!" The man at the counter has short hair, beautifully dark eyes, and a huge smile. "Bulgogi?"

Ben smiles right back, his dimples practically putting my eyes out, and they're not even turned on me. "Absolutely. My friend here wants to try the bibimbap."

"Good choice," the man says. "And did you say your friend, or your *girlfriend?* Because if she's just your friend, I may throw in some crispy tofu along with my number." He wiggles his eyebrows. "I'm not only cute, I own this place."

"Doesn't your mom own it?" Ben asks.

The guy waves his hand. "Potato, pohtahto. It's better not to get hung up on those kinds of details."

Ben sideswiped the question, which is odd. It's not like there's any world in which I'm his girlfriend. It should have been an easy one.

"Is the fried tofu good?" I ask.

"It's so good you'll come beg *me* for my phone number," the guy says.

"We'll add that to the order, and I'll pay for it." Ben turns toward me. "Then it's *me* you'll be begging, right?"

I can't help my laugh. "I'm pretty sure I already got your phone number yesterday."

"So she's *not* your girlfriend." The guy sets two glasses down and leans on the counter. "Fair game, then."

"You two are ridiculous." I snatch my glass and spin on my heel, busying myself with choosing a soda. Dr. Pepper, maybe? I should just drink water. I've been planning to cut soda out of my diet for a long time.

"You still like Dr. Pepper?" Ben shoves his glass under the icemaker and then hits the Dr. Pepper button.

How did he remember that? "I'm really that boring?"

"Not boring," he says. "It's been my favorite ever since you pointed out how much better it was than regular Coke."

I give up on the water thing and fill my cup as soon as he's done. "I still drink it." It's not like refusing to admit it's my favorite means anything. I think my brain is currently sitting crooked inside my skull.

"Want to sit in the corner? There's less foot traffic over here."

"Sure." I follow him to the table in the very back.

Almost before I've sat down, he starts asking me questions about the plan we formulated yesterday. I explain how I've fleshed it out, and the ideas my boss had to make it a little more viable.

"You spent a lot of time thinking about this," he says. "How did you know my uncle would turn us down?"

I shrug. "I didn't. But it's our job to be prepared no matter which turn the situation takes."

He sighs. "Isn't it kind of tiresome, always planning for the worst case scenario?"

"When you don't plan, it hurts more." I can't help thinking of the day of prom—and the week after. That was a hard hit, and I was utterly unprepared.

"I suppose so."

"I'm sorry about your uncle," I say. "I'm not sure whether I've said that. I know you and your mother were both hoping he'd come through."

"You think we'll be able to move past this?"

"On a corporate level?" I nod. "People don't care nearly as much as they should. They may be outraged for a day or even a week. Some of them might hold onto that fury for a month, but eventually they'll circle back around. They'll go to the repair shop that has their information on file, the one that gives them a ride back home, the one they've used before, or the one that's closest to their house. People are so self-interested that they don't hold on to anything that inconveniences them."

"Wow, you're a real optimist."

I shrug. "Depends on your perspective. In this instance, it helps you, right? I mean, you don't want your business to fail."

"I'm just tired of my dad getting away with everything. The more time you spend talking about how we'll polish up our image, the more I think about punching him in the face. Someone should do something—he should have to pay. Don't you think?"

"The world isn't fair," I say. "Rich people don't live the same way. You'll only lose sleep by obsessing over that."

"At least one good thing came out of this," he says.

"What?" I look up at him.

And that's when they bring our food.

Of course.

My life always has exactly this kind of timing.

The guy who took our orders is the person who brings us our plates as well, all three of them on a tray. "Here's the bibimbap." He sets it in front of me and it's way prettier than I envisioned. It's a large bowl with several colors of vegetables in piles, and a big section with steaming beef. Then there's bright red sauce spread back and forth over the top of it.

"What's in the sauce?" I ask.

"It's a secret," the guy says, "but I swear you'll love it." He points at the napkin below the bowl. "When you're craving more, that's my number. I'll even deliver." He winks.

"Get out of here," Ben says.

The guy grins as he places the tofu and the bulgogi on the table. "Not all of us own a huge company. We have to work with what we have." He shrugs and then walks away.

"That guy." Ben shakes his head.

"If it's as good as you say, maybe I should call him."

Ben picks up a pair of chopsticks. "You'll be pretty busy on this for a while, won't you?"

"I haven't even gotten a signed agreement of representation yet," I say.

"We can fix that as soon as we get back to the office." Ben grins. "I need you to keep helping out. You're the only good part of my day right now."

"Why didn't you marry Jennifer?" I blurt. I have to close my hand around a fork to keep from covering my own mouth. *Why did I ask that? What's wrong with me?*

"How did you even know we were engaged?"

"Let's see." I hold up my index finger. "Facebook posts from mutual friends."

"Right." He looks a little embarrassed about that.

"Also, Mary called me." I hold up my second finger.

"How did she know?" he asks, looking almost horrified.

"Same," I say. "I assume."

"Duh."

I hold up a third finger. "And finally, I saw it in the paper." Or rather, Mary forwarded me the article about their upcoming wedding when she found it, and I blacked out the day on my calendar. I might have gotten tipsy that night. Luckily I don't blurt any of that out.

"I should never have gotten engaged in the first place," he says. "I never loved her." His eyes widen. "That was an embarrassingly private thing to say." He sighs. "Her parents live next door to my parents."

"Oh, I remember." The heat in my cheeks warns me that I'm blushing, but at least this time, Ben looks equally flustered.

"I'm not sure I ever apologized for how all of that went down."

I shake my head. "Stop. I should never have asked. I didn't mean to open that can of worms. Obviously you and I were always a stupid idea—"

"Why?" He looks genuinely perplexed.

I can't help laughing. "Let's focus on the issue at hand, huh? I think—"

Ben reaches across the table and catches my hand. "That's what I'm trying to do. You have no idea how embarrassed I was at first, when I saw you there at the press conference. I should've known you weren't there to laugh at us or to twist the knife. You clearly came to help us. You've shifted and reconfigured and bent over back-wards at every turn to improve my life. Just like always."

"Ben—"

"I proposed to Jennifer because my parents wouldn't

leave me alone about it, and she was so excited about our future together. No matter what happened, she kept getting flung back at me. She's smart and pretty, and I figured, why keep fighting?" His shoulders slump. "What a stupid reason to propose. I didn't even buy the ring. My dad had the jewelry store send one over."

That's. . .maybe one of the saddest things I've ever heard. "She deserved better."

He meets my eyes, his own quite shocked. "She did, yeah."

"No matter how dreamy the guy is, no girl imagines a future where the guy's forced to marry her."

"Her dad owns car dealerships, you know. A bunch of them."

"I forgot that."

"Her dad and mine work together, still. In fact, I saw her a few weeks ago. She's happily married to an accountant at her dad's firm. They have a kid on the way."

"Well, that's good. If she's happy."

"I think she is."

"Look, Ben, I know that ten years ago—"

"It wasn't quite ten, you know. Our reunion's coming up this summer. I signed up to go at first, and then remembered you wouldn't be going, being two years behind. So I cancelled."

A few times in my life, I've fallen and hit my backside really hard, and once a soccer ball whammed right into my chest. When stuff like that happens, the wind's knocked out of my body, and I can't breathe. That's what happens right now, only without the blunt force trauma.

He wanted to see me again?

Does he regret what happened? But he's the one who didn't call. He's the one whose fault it is. . .

"I can't do this," I say.

But that's a lie. I've dreamed about Ben telling me he

likes me for *years*. I've dreamed about it recently. Sometimes, when I imagine a scene just like this, I lie in bed after waking with my eyes closed, wishing I'd fall back to sleep and relive it one more time.

And now he's in front of me, with both his dimples, with his athletic build, and no ring on his finger, and he's telling me he didn't marry Jennifer, and that he wanted to see me this summer, and I'm telling him what? That I can't? Can't what? Can't be normal? Can't let something good happen?

But maybe that's my problem.

I can't imagine, no matter how many times I dream about it, that Ben would really like me, that we could ever ride off into the sunset.

He's like Saturn. Beautiful, unique, otherworldly.

I'm a trash rock. Space junk.

We're not even on the same scale of measurement.

"What can't you do?" Ben asks. "Eat the bibimbap? Try the fried tofu? Help me on this case?" He leans closer. "Or are you saying that if I ask you out right now, you'll turn me down flat? Do you have some firm policy against dating clients?"

"I, I mean—" We probably do, actually. "Yes. The firm won't let me date you."

"And I'm guessing since you sought me out, that you need this account?" He looks pained.

I nod.

"Alright. Well."

"We should make sure we're on the same page with our game plan. Then we can put together the press release and get things moving."

"Right."

But Ben looks as wrecked as I feel.

❧ *9* ❧

ADDY

****TEN YEARS AGO****

Mary and I are rummaging through my closet for the fourth time, hoping that something viable will miraculously emerge, when Mom knocks on the doorframe.

"Still panicking over prom?" Her expression is compassionate. I told her weeks ago, but I also understand we don't have money for a fancy dress.

"It's fine, Mom. I told you. I'll figure something out."

"You could put the plaid skirt with that white shirt." Mom reaches for the skirt.

Oh good. The richest guy at school asked me to prom, and I can go dressed as a Catholic private school kid with a slightly-too-small plaid skirt.

I know we're lucky that mom makes enough to pay for necessities. I'm also grateful that grandma and grandpa pitch in when things get unbearably tight, but some days I don't feel super lucky. Today is one of those days.

"Prom's tomorrow, Mom. Mary came over to brainstorm."

"I'm here right at the perfect time, then." Mom sighs. "Because if you didn't tell me that the plaid skirt idea was stupid, you're really desperate."

Of course I'm desperate. I'm a sophomore going to prom with a senior, and my best option for a dress is. . .I don't have a single one.

Mom's beaming when she reaches behind my door and pulls out a bag. "I realized when I was in the attic looking for—you know what? It doesn't matter. The point is that the Christmas pillows I bought with my bonus still had the tags on them. It was a little over 90 days, but the lady at Ross took pity on me and. . ." She whips something slinky out of the bag and extends it toward me.

I take it from her greedily, my hopes soaring.

"It was originally over a hundred dollars," Mom says.

It's a champagne colored sheath dress, and I can barely believe my eyes. Until I put in on, that is. The dress itself isn't so bad—it's even the right size. But someone stupid dolled it up with cascading flowers sewn on from the bottom of my bust on the right side, all the way down to my hip. The embellishments are bright white flowers that are almost blinding against the champagne fabric. The material they're made with wasn't the highest quality to begin with, and possibly from being on the rack for so long, or possibly from the heat of a warehouse, the flowers have drooped.

They look like blobs of melted marshmallows sliding down the side of my body.

Ugh.

It takes every ounce of my energy to convince my mother that I'm absolutely giddy about her brilliant find, but the second she leaves, I start bawling, and I can't stop. Not even when Ben calls—Mary tells him I'm taking a shower, which is ridiculous. Who takes a shower at five in the afternoon?

It takes me almost half an hour to calm down, and I'm not sure I would have, except for Mary's idea.

"What if we took the flowers off?"

I wipe at my face. "If we did what?"

"The dress isn't so bad. It's the flowers that ruin it."

I stand up and force myself to look at it again in the mirror that hangs on the back of my door. She's right.

It takes us another thirty minutes to rip the flowers off. The dress really doesn't look so bad—it hugs my figure, and while I'm not exactly curvy, I don't look terrible. It's a bit simple—a plain, polyester sheath dress— but it's not embarrassing.

Unfortunately, every spot where a flower was attached puckers, and now it looks like the side of my body's covered with boils underneath my dress or something.

Mary starts laughing.

My steadfast, devoted friend is laughing at me.

"What's so funny?"

"It's just that I was so jealous that you were going to prom." She collapses onto my bed.

I flop down onto my desk chair. "I know. Ridiculous, right? Me, going to prom? And it's not like you'd be any better off."

Tears are streaming down her face now. "Oh, I'd totally be worse. I can see it now. My dad would save the day with. . .a box of trash bags. You and I would have to fashion me something out of Glad bags and duct tape swiped from the auto repair shop on the corner."

Her laugh is contagious, always has been, and now I can't keep from laughing either. It's always better to suffer with a friend, but I still have no plan. "What am I going to do?"

"A shawl?" Now she's hooting. "Ooh, I know. We could cut up this sweater and make you a cape." She reaches for the sweater Mom found at Goodwill last year for an ugly sweater competition at school. The sequins and beads all over the front of it outline a nutcracker, a reindeer, and a snowman. I suppose if you can't come up with a cohesive single theme for a sweater, it makes sense to vomit everything on it at the same time.

"Wait." Mary's staring at the front of the sweater like inspiration has stuck. "I have an idea." She lifts her eyes slowly.

"What?"

"It could be amazing." The corner of her mouth turns up.

"Or?"

"Or it could totally backfire, and you could be stuck going to prom in a plaid skirt."

I shrug. "It's not like I have a lot to lose."

She rummages around in my drawer until she finds the sewing kit she gave me last year for Christmas. The one I've never touched. Mary's a whiz with almost everything, but she's been mending their clothes for years. She clearly paid much more attention in home economics than I did.

My darling friend stays up until nearly three in the morning doing the impossible. We sleep in super late on Saturday, and by the time we wake up, eat breakfast after lunch time, and I shower, I realize we don't have a lot of time for me to get ready for prom.

Mary waits in my room while I dive into the shower and she's got my makeup all laid out, as well as two different options for shoes, when I return in a towel.

"You can go punk rock." She points at my Converse. "Or you can go elegant." She points at my mom's black pumps.

School kid or soccer mom would be more accurate descriptions, but Mary always puts a positive spin on almost everything.

My mom taps on the doorframe again, reminding me

that I left it hanging open. "Are you sure you don't want me to do your hair?"

"It's so nice of you to offer, but I'm sure." After years and years of Mom doing my hair for church, I am absolutely positive I don't want her anywhere near my hair today. I can see how it would turn out already—two French braids starting at the base of my neck, moving upward so they're 'sophisticated,' and then twisted together on top of my head.

I would look seven years old. I suppress my shudder.

"You're really just curling it? That's it?" She frowns. "But I looked up some stuff online and—"

"Mom, really." She always means so well that I feel terrible turning her down.

It takes almost an hour, but my baby fine hair is finally all dry and curled. Mary's starting on my makeup when Mom returns. "I looked some things up online, and how about if—"

She freezes. "Whoa!"

I should have prepared her or something.

"What in the world happened to the dress?"

Mary leaps to her feet. "Well, the thing is—"

"It looks *amazing!*" Mom pulls me up to a standing position as well and turns me around like I'm a ballerina on a jewelry box. "Who did this?" She looks at me.

As if I could ever embroider flowers and butterflies, embellished with artfully placed sequins and beads.

"I watched a few YouTube videos," Mary says. "It really wasn't super hard."

"Super hard? This is breathtaking." My mom's eyes actually tear up. "I can't let you go, now."

"What?" *Please, please, please be kidding.* Mom has a really odd sense of humor.

"When you were just a kid, it was alright," Mom says. "But now you look like Cinderella."

At least it's a joke, but she's exaggerating big time. "I'm glad you like it, but it's really—"

Mom pulls me tightly against her. "I really hope you have a wonderful time, Addy. It's been a hard year."

She's not wrong about that, but I can tell that Mom's exuberance is making Mary sad. Her mother left a long time ago—to Mary this really is a Cinderella story. A mother who would exchange pillows for a dress? A senior asking me to be his date? I'll be dancing in this amazing dress, thanks to her, and she'll be stuck at home making hotdogs for Trudy again.

"Thank you, Mary. Without you—" I choke up.

No matter how tonight goes, I'm lucky to have the mother and friend that I have.

I try to remember that when the bell rings an hour later.

When I open the door, Ben's already smiling. "Are you ready?"

"Excuse me, young man, but we haven't even been introduced." Mom lifts her chin. "You'd better do a good job convincing me that you'll be a gentleman."

Ben doesn't cringe. He doesn't balk. He's not even awkward. His smile widens, and he steps inside, his broad shoulders—clad in a perfectly tailored tux—barely fitting through the doorway. "My name is Ben Newberg, Mrs. Thorley. I can't tell you how delighted I am that you're allowing your daughter to come with me to prom."

Mom blinks.

"When I met her at Camp K.E.E.P., I knew right away that something was special about her. I don't think a day has gone by that she hasn't said something I needed to hear."

"Oh. Well, that's very nice. You'll have her home by eleven? On the dot?"

Ben's mouth drops open.

"Mom, prom doesn't even end until eleven, and it's downtown."

"Oh. Well, twelve, then?"

Ben nods.

"Great," Mom says. "Great."

"See you later," I say.

"I'm totally waiting here until you come home," Mary says. "Have so much fun!"

Ben offers me his hand, and I take it, our fingers sliding easily together. What's not easy is how it makes me feel—the pressure of his hand against mine causes my heart to hammer inside my chest. As I follow him out to his big black truck, I realize it's not just the pressure of his hand. It's not just some kind of physical chemistry. Since Mom won't let me date, this is the first time I've been around him, really. We don't share classes or the same lunch period. We don't see each other at school. Other than talking to him on the phone, I haven't really seen him since camp.

Until now.

And he's claimed my hand as if it's his, and he's leading me to his car. He walks around to the passenger side and opens the door for me. I'm honestly a little disappointed when I remember that Mike and his date, Rebecca, a really nice senior with bright red hair, are waiting inside.

"Addy!" Mike's always the life of the party, so I'm happy he's here, but. . .

"Mike! And Mike's date!" I know her name is Rebecca, but since we've never met, it would be kind of weird for me to use it.

"It's Rebecca," she says. "So nice to finally meet you, Addy. I've heard good things."

"Oh?" Now I'm nervous. Who told her things, and what exactly did they say?

"We told her all about your keen sense of fashion," Mike says, "and she's dying to get her hands on some boots just like yours."

"Maybe a size smaller, from what the guys say."

I should be annoyed, or feel attacked, but I don't. Mike has that effect on people. If it were anyone else, I might feel picked on, but Mike would never make fun of me behind my back. "I think eBay is your only hope." I can't help my smirk.

Ben climbs in and starts the truck. "I'm not sure we'd ever have become friends if it weren't for those boots. I should probably be hunting for a pair for myself."

"Oh, I'll be happy to loan you mine any time," I say. "I bet they're about your size."

He laughs. "Probably true."

The rest of prom passes a bit like a dream. I worried that I'd walk inside and people would point or mock or jeer. But being with Ben is like an all-access pass. If the other girls are thinking mean things, with his arm around me, they don't dare imply them, much less say them out loud. He's far too sharp to miss even subtle snubs. And if Ben wasn't enough, Mike makes it pretty clear that we're friends as well, even snaking me away for not one, but two dances.

"Ben's a lucky guy," Mike says. "If he hadn't called you first, you might be here with me instead."

"Oh, please," I say. "Rebecca's way too good for you."

He laughs. "Probably true, but I've always been someone who aims high."

"Thank you," I say.

His eyebrows draw together. "For what?"

"For being my friend, even though I'm an awkward sophomore."

"You have the coolest dress here. You're unique and funny and smart. The only complaint I have is that you seem to use the wrong word a lot. When you get home tonight, I have some homework for you."

"Oh?"

"Look up the word awkward. When you take the SAT, you'll want to know the real meaning of that one for sure." He leans a little closer. "It doesn't apply to you, Addy. Not at all."

Ben grabs Mike's arm and hauls him backward a bit. "Too close, Mikey. She's *my* date."

Both of them laugh, and Mike shakes Ben's hand off and straightens his tux. "Not all of us own our evening wear, Sir Ben. Perhaps go a little lighter on the yanking and twisting. I don't want to lose my deposit."

"You own your tux?" I can't help asking, once Ben has swept me back onto the dance floor.

"Do you feel suitably bad for me?"

"Huh?"

"What guy on earth wants to own his own tux?" He sighs. "You only own a tux if your parents drag you to fancy events far too often."

I think about that. I didn't even have a dress suitable for something like this, and if Mary hadn't been willing to work on this all night, instead of a long line of compliments, I'd be subjected to a litany of giggles and scoffs. "How bored are you tonight, exactly? On a scale of one to ten, maybe."

Ben pulls me closer, his arm tightening on my back. "Maybe a five or a six?"

"A five?" My voice is just a tad too shrill to be passed off as a joke. "Are you kidding?"

His grin is lopsided. "Why would I be kidding? We've been here for hours now."

"You don't like dancing?"

"It's overrated." He pulls me a little bit closer, still.

Our bodies are touching from my hip all the way to our chests, almost.

"You're pretty good at it," I say softly.

"Again, thanks to my parents dragging me to stupid parties."

"Well, I appreciate your misery." I bite my lip. "But I won't lie and say that I'm happy to hear tonight rated a five or six."

"I suppose if I factor in the company, it would move up a little."

"To what?"

He shrugs. "Maybe a seven?"

"What would I have to do to get it to an eight?"

He tilts his head. "Hmm."

"Dance on the table?"

He shakes his head. "No, that's too obvious."

"Drink an entire bowl of punch in under sixty seconds?"

"Spiked?" He arches one eyebrow.

I slug his shoulder.

"I have a better idea." His eyes are looking directly at my mouth.

And it's like all the oxygen in the room has evacuated the premises. I still manage to squeak out a few words. "You do?"

He nods, his eyes never leaving my mouth.

"Which is?" I drag in a ragged breath.

"I think you can guess." His head dips a little lower, and his eyelids lower until he looks half asleep.

"Why would you make me guess?" I inhale sharply. "I mean, it's not like we're playing twenty questions." Before I couldn't think what to say, and now I'm babbling.

"We could play twenty something." His head lowers just a bit more.

The song changes.

It's like Ben doesn't even notice. Instead of couples moving together, individuals crowd the dance floor around us. Someone bumps me in the back, and I fly forward.

Ben's head closes the gap, his lips pressing against mine.

In the middle of the dance floor.

With half the senior class gathered around us.

His hand tightens between my shoulder blades, forcing me even closer to him. His lips slant over mine, and my heart races, and I forget about everything but Ben. And his mouth. And his insouciant smile. I go up on my tiptoes and Ben makes a weird kind of whimpering sound.

And then I realize that someone is cheering.

Because of us.

I rock back on my heels, and Ben releases me, both of us panting and a little dazed.

But the hoots and hollers and shouts and cheers wake me right up. How could we have had our first kiss on the dance floor? In the middle of prom?

My only explanation is that we were wrapped in some kind of couple bubble, and neither of us cared where we were. I should remember this the next time my parents tell me that dating is a bad idea. *Not* dating is what led me to have this bizarrely public first kiss.

Ugh.

"Ben and Maddy, sitting in a tree—"

"It's *Addy*," Mike shouts.

I almost laugh at how absurd it is for him to correct someone who's singing a mocking, elementary school song about us.

"Do you want to go?" Ben asks.

I nod.

"Mike—find a ride."

Ben's best friend doesn't even argue. He just salutes us as we walk out the door, hand in hand again. I do notice Jennifer's face as we walk past her—it's not anger. It's not even hurt feelings.

She's shocked.

I can't even blame her. In my wildest dreams, I would never have imagined coming to prom tonight, or kissing Ben. But I'd certainly never have thought he'd drag me out early by the hand, as if he plans to consume me or something.

Consume.

My mouth goes dry. *What does he plan to do?*

When Ben turns the truck on, the clock on the dash says ten oh three. "We have two hours." His voice isn't flat, but it's not normal either. I can't put a finger on what exactly makes it sound so strange.

"What do you want to do?"

He laughs. "I'm a teenage boy. Don't ask stuff like that. The better question is what *should* we do?"

"If you take me home, my mom will see you off before you can say 'teenage boy.'"

He chuckles, which is a totally different sound than his laugh. It's low, it's casual, and I wish I could hear it over and over and over forever. He turns then, his hand lifting toward my face. His fingers gently brush my hair back and tuck it behind my ear. "I could kiss you all night. I could stare at you for just as long, too. But none of those things feel as important as learning every single thing there is to know about you."

"Then I vote we go to IHOP and get milkshakes."

He grins. "That's a perfect plan."

So that's exactly what we do. I pick a strawberry shake, and he goes for chocolate. We talk for an hour before he pays the check, and then we chat for another half hour after that. Eventually, he reluctantly follows me back out to the truck. "It feels like you really are Cinderella and we're running out of time." He groans. "Why can't you date, again?"

I climb into the truck, but instead of walking around to the drivers' side, he leans toward me.

"I *like* you, Addy. I can't stop thinking about you. I want to talk to you all the time. I want to touch you every minute. I want to hear what you think about everything." His hands drop down on my forearms and he brushes a kiss against my forehead. "I want to see you every single day before I have to leave."

The words drop between us like a rock in a still pond.

He leaves for college in a few months. I hadn't even thought about it. Of course he does—he's a senior.

"I don't want you to go."

He freezes. "I leave right when you can finally date. What a stupid cosmic joke."

I laugh as if it's funny, but the sound is too high, too brittle. "We're misaligned. We don't fit."

"You fit with me." He sounds so certain. "Couldn't you tell tonight? I'm happier when we're together."

"If a five is happier, then I'm not so sure—"

He barks a laugh. "I was so full of it, trying to sound cool. Tonight was a ten, and kissing you bumped it even higher. I'm not sure up to what. The only thing better than dancing all night with you was drinking shakes at that IHOP. I wanted you all to myself." He frowns. "But will your mom be mad when she hears I took you to get food?"

I hadn't even thought about it. Honestly, it's so much better than what I *thought* he might be planning that she should be relieved. But it'll be safer for both of us if she never finds out.

"I ought to go inside."

"Can you call me?" he asks. "Once you're inside?"

"You want me to call you at midnight?"

"I want you to call me anytime."

My heart flutters again. "Okay."

Which is why I'm on the phone with him, talking about my favorite color of skittles—red—when he says, "Oh my—Jennifer, what are you doing here? And what are you wea—"

And then the phone line cuts out.

I glance at the clock. It's one-thirty in the morning. Ben was at his house, just like I was at mine. And then Jennifer showed up, and then he shouted. . .and hung up.

I call him back three times.

He doesn't answer.

Ten minutes later, he finally calls me. I pick it up so fast I wonder if he knows I've been frantic over here. "What just happened?"

He sighs. "You don't want to know."

"Actually, I really do," I say. "Jennifer was at your house? I thought you were in your bedroom. Did you go outside or something?"

"I was in my bedroom." His voice is the flattest I've ever heard.

"And?"

"And Jennifer's family has a key to our house—they know the security code, too. She just barged into my room."

"In the middle of the night?"

"Naked."

My brain decides to take a little vacation. Nothing processes for a full five seconds. Then I finally catch up. "What?!"

"I sent her right back out—believe me. I have no idea what she was thinking."

He may not know, but I have a few ideas.

"It's the middle of the night." He sounds indignant.

"Why did it take you ten minutes to call me back?"

He's very quiet. Too quiet.

"Ben?"

"My dad heard us," he whispers. "And—"

"Oh, no. Did he freak out?"

Ben makes a strangled sound. "Not exactly."

What?

"He might have tried to convince me to keep her here."

This time it's my turn to choke.

"My dad's got a strange perspective, and he likes Jennifer's family. Look, I took care of it, okay? I swear, she will never do anything that stupid again."

What am I doing? Ben Newberg is the kind of guy every girl wants. The head cheerleader of our school shows up at his house, naked, in the middle of the night, and his dad is totally cool with it.

Meanwhile, I just ate a stale bag of Cheetos I found at the bottom of my laundry basket while we were talking on the phone. And my mom returned Christmas pillows to buy me a prom dress, and that was the nicest thing she has done for me this year. She loved those pillows.

We have no business even being friends.

"Addy, I know what you're thinking."

I doubt that very much.

"You think Jennifer is a problem, but believe me, I'm not into her at all. You're nothing like her, and that's one of the things I like most."

I'm a novelty to him, something new and unique in his life. I think I've known that for a while. From the boots to the sequined dress, to the poor family. I'm something new that he's never tried.

"Promise me something, Addy."

"Okay." It almost feels like I'm floating right now, everything feels so surreal.

"Promise that when I call you tomorrow, and the day after, and the day after that, you'll pick up. You won't give up on us."

"I promise," I say.

I really mean it. As much as this feels like a fairy tale, as much as I worry that tomorrow, all that will be left is a glass slipper, I *long* for it to be real.

But I'm not surprised when he doesn't call the next day. Or the one after that. Or any day thereafter. I'm not surprised at all, because in real life, Cinderella doesn't get the prince. She moves on with her sad little life, washing dishes, and talking to animals. The prince marries some rich daughter of a lord—because that's what they do.

※ 10 ※

BEN

The last time my dad summoned me to a meeting, I was about to leave for college. I was a kid—I barely needed to shave. That day, we argued fiercely. He told me that Addy Thorley was a disaster. He told me that her father had come to him, mentioned that I was taking her to prom, and pitched an idea for a business.

"So what?" I asked. "So her dad wanted to partner with you. Is that a crime?"

"His business plan was almost criminally bad," Dad said. "And he kept going on and on—he had no idea his idea was terrible."

"Dad, I like Addy. Like, I *like* her." I frowned. "I'm not even sure she likes her dad. So you certainly don't have to like him for me to like her."

"You're eighteen," Dad said. "You don't know up from down. You should like Jennifer—her dad is brilliant. Her dad is a friend. Her dad would never beg me, like literally drop down on his hands and knees and *beg* me to give him money."

I argued with him for a long time, but in the end, Dad won.

He always won.

Because he held all the cards.

I hadn't bothered applying for a scholarship to school —not that I'd have gotten one if I had—because I knew Dad would pay for UCLA. I'd seen the balance in my college fund, so why even bother trying for scholarships? There were plenty of kids, like Addy, who needed that scholarship money.

But that left me stuck. I couldn't defy him, not without wrecking my own future. I threw in the towel, figuring I could always ask Addy out later.

Only, later never really came. UCLA consumed me, and then when I returned home, Jennifer was *everywhere.* Addy had gone out of state for school, I heard, and anyway, I realized that a girl like her was unlikely to forgive me for not calling her.

I didn't even have the guts to dump her.

What would I have said if I called her four years later? *My dad told me that if I dated you, he'd cut me off? He said your dad is a beggar? He can't stand you, and called you a gold digger? I'm such a loser that I couldn't even change his mind?*

This time, when Dad summons me, I'm not a kid. I'm almost thirty years old. I know my dad's a bully of the worst kind.

And I'm sick of being pushed around.

Part of me hopes, when I realize Dad has convened a board meeting, that Uncle Chris has changed his mind.

"I imagine you two know why you're here today." He glances between Uncle Chris and me. "Just to make sure no one's confused, I'll say it. Vivian's divorcing me, and my lawyer says I should assume she'll go after partial ownership in all the businesses." He drops a stack of papers on the table in the conference room. "I want to make sure we're all on the same page if we're deposed or asked to answer interrogatories. I can't have her taking my companies. Not one iota of them. I started all but one before we married, and I've grown them all myself. You two can both attest to that, I assume?"

The day after he almost destroyed the company with his illegal and unethical practices, he calls Uncle Chris and me into the office and asks us to *lie* for him? It's too much. "Mom worked long hours. Maybe as many as you."

Dad's jaw clenches. "As a secretary, as a receptionist, as a clerk."

"She said when you met, and even when I was born, you only had one location, one auto repair shop, the one on State Street."

"You should know better than to believe a thing she says," Dad says.

"Do you mean a thing you say?" I stare at him, resisting the urge to drop my eyes. "I really ought to stay here and let you unfold your entire plan to me. I ought to pry and push and prod. But I can't do it—I can't do anything you would do, as it turns out."

"What does that mean?" Dad leans toward me, his eyes flashing.

"You're a liar. You're a cheat. And you're not someone I want anything to do with."

"Even if the court goes insane and awards your mother partial ownership of this company, up to half of what I own, I'll still be the CEO," Dad says. "You would be wise to remember that."

"That's not true," I say. "I own seventeen percent. I spoke to the lawyer this morning. And that means you own barely over forty percent. So if Mom takes half of that—"

"You're missing some vital information," Uncle Chris

says. "I came over this morning with paperwork of my own." He shoves an envelope toward me.

I rip the document out and scan it. "I don't know what this is."

"Your Uncle Chris is loyal," Dad says. "I long since repaid him for his original investment, and now, in my time of trouble, he's signed his interest in the company over to me, in trust, so it's very clearly separate property —a gift from family—and so no matter what the Court does when your mother tells her sob story, I'll still own a controlling interest in my own company."

"But if—"

"It's checkmate, son," Dad says. "Now, if you're done throwing your little tantrum, let's start talking about our next steps."

"A tantrum?" I snort. "Was that what you called it ten years ago, when you told me to dump Addy Thorley?"

Dad blinks. "What are you talking about?"

"I took Addy to prom," I say, "and the next day, you told me I could never talk to her again. I called her over and over, but she was never home. When I asked you about it, you told me to let it go. You told me that her dad was pathetic, and I was better off without her."

"Ah, right. One of the many times I had to save my pathetic son from himself."

I shove my chair backward as I stand up. "I didn't want your help then, and I certainly don't want it now."

"I was trying to spare your feelings—I didn't even tell you the whole story."

"Excuse me?"

"That girl's dad came and begged me to invest in his company."

"You told me that."

"When I refused, repeatedly, he dropped down on his knees and cried about how he was going to lose his house." Dad's lip curls. "He was worried his second wife might leave him—not even his daughter's mother. He was using a connection to that girl you took to the dance to try and save his other family. What kind of person does that?"

"Dad—"

"Listen for a moment. This is the girl you're upset that I separated you from. A girl whose father would crawl into another man's office and bawl like a child, trying to trade on a connection to a girl he's already abandoned to save his second family. He laid all his personal business out to a complete stranger." He shakes his head in disgust.

"That was years ago—"

"The saddest part is that I didn't have control over my own son. I knew that even when I told you not to call her, not to contact her, that you'd ignore me. So I paid him to make sure that you and that girl would have no future contact."

My entire body stiffens. "You did what?"

"Guess what it cost me to ensure your bright future? He charged a lot, since he had to pay his ex-wife to get her to comply." His smile is so superior and so condescending that it makes me sick.

"You paid Addy Thorley's father to make sure that every time I called, she'd be unavailable?"

"Not only that, he got her mother on board. It was brilliant of me, right?" Dad's just preening now. "I mean, I told you that your entire future was on the line. I told you I wouldn't pay for your college, and I knew you well enough to know you'd call her anyway. That's how pathetic you were—how much of your mother is in you." He snorts. "You can see why it's so important, that you marry the right girl. It's basic biology. It doesn't matter that you're my son. If you have half of your genetic material from someone else, someone weak, someone stupid, it impacts you. Your mother wrecked you—I couldn't very well let that pathetic idiot's DNA further corrupt the family line."

"You think that his begging and his crying makes him somehow less than you?"

"It makes him a loser," Dad says. "For five grand, I was able to separate the two of you forever. Tell me that wasn't a bargain."

"You're even worse than I realized."

"Every good thing in your life has come as a result of me," Dad says. "Your good looks, your education, your skill, and even your success at business. All gifts from me."

I realize that he's right. I've lived my entire life according to the dictates of Dad's whims. Even now, no matter what I do, I'm playing his game, and he's still holding all the cards.

That's why I'll always lose.

Mom's divorcing him, but dad and I aren't married. I don't have the luxury of going to court and filing for a formal separation. I can't tell the world that I'm not his son, or insist that I'm not his blood. But there is one thing I can do that sends the same message.

It's far past time for me to do it.

"Dad," I say. "Listen closely. I'd hate if I was unclear. I want to make sure you know exactly how I feel on each point." I pause for dramatic effect. "You're a terrible father. You're an even worse husband. And that man you said is pathetic? He's the perfect example of just how bad you are. He was willing to come into the office of a total stranger, and he was willing to crawl on his hands and knees and beg you for money, no matter how awful you were, no matter how hard that was, because he would do literally anything for his family—even if it's his second.

Maybe losing the first taught him the value of what he'd lost. Who knows?"

Dad tries to interrupt me, like always, but I'm not letting him, not this time.

"He may not be a business maven like you, and he may actually be pathetic. But he's still ten times the person you are." I lean forward until our faces are only a foot or so apart. "Because of your repeated inadequacies as a father, because of your abuse to both me and Mom, and because of your selfish and misguided interventions into my life at literally every point, I'm leaving this company, this office, and this life. In a simple phrase that I think you'll understand: I quit everything to do with you."

11

BEN

I am unemployed.

I alienated my father.

I have no plans for the future.

This may not be my finest moment, but it *feels* like it is. Which is probably why I call Addy.

"Hello?"

Her voice is like sunlight in the darkest night.

It's like manna in the wilderness.

Or like water in the middle of a drought.

"It's me," I say. "Ben."

"I knew it was you." Her voice is light. "I have this secret weapon on my phone—I think it's called *Caller ID*." She clears her throat. "I have the retainer agreement all filled out and ready to go. Should I email it over? Or would it be better if I brought it over in person?"

As if my brain was on some kind of strike before, I suddenly remember something she said. She needs the Newberg Auto account—that's why she hunted me down. She needs to bring clients to her firm, or she won't get the promotion she deserves.

And I just ensured there's no way she'll ever get Dad's business.

There's no chance my dad won't remember the name Addy Thorley now. Why didn't I sign her contract yesterday? I'm sure Dad would have found some way around it even if I had, so maybe it wouldn't have mattered.

All that work she just did, and I ruined it all with my way-too-late epiphany.

"Uh, yeah. About that."

"What's wrong?" Her voice isn't light anymore.

"I just had a meeting with my dad, and he—is there any way you can meet me? Maybe for breakfast or something?"

"If it's bad news, I'd rather hear it now," she says. "I'm not the kind of person who needs to be let down easy. In fact, it was perfect how you did it last time—just not calling at all."

Oh, man. "Actually, I got some new information on that today, too. When I met with my dad, he told me that he actually *paid* your father to make sure your mother wouldn't let you talk to me. I did try calling a few times—"

"He did *what?*"

"Did I mention my father's a terrible person?" I exhale. "Look, to be honest, my dad and I got into a big argument. I got really upset about how he's been treating my mom and how he essentially forced you out of my life a decade ago."

"And you quit your job."

How did she know that? "Uh, yeah. I did."

"It was the right thing to do." But she sounds as glum as I've ever heard her.

"I think so too," I say. "But—"

"You have a lot going on right now," she says. "Don't worry about me or the contract. It's no big deal, truly.

Figure out your next steps, and if you have any more major problems or know anyone who does, reach out to me. I don't live at home anymore, and I promise that I'll always answer your call."

She just made a joke. Maybe that's encouraging.

And then I hear the dial tone.

The hanging up thing is *not* so promising. I'm about to call her back and insist that she see me when my phone rings. I hope it's Addy—but it's not. It's my mom. "Hello?"

"*You quit your job?*"

"Mom, hi, it's nice to hear from you as well."

"He wins if you leave, don't you see that?"

"I don't agree with you," I say. "I think that he wins as long as I'm still marching to his tune."

"Principles are nice, but they don't pay the bills," Mom says. "What's your plan now that you're unemployed?"

"I'm going to start my own auto repair shop." The idea literally just popped into my head, and it might be predominantly fueled by my desire to stick it to my dad, but it doesn't feel like a bad one. I have all the contacts. I know how the business works. I even know which areas Dad was thinking of expanding into next. "I'm going to beat him at his own game."

"You'll lose." Mom's voice is half angry, half resigned.

"Thanks for the vote of confidence."

"Remember what happens when you play Monopoly with your dad?"

"He always wins."

"He cheats, Ben. You can't beat someone who cheats, and he does it in business, too. You can't try and beat him at his own game. He won't go easy on you. In his mind, crushing you will send you back to him, which is what's best for you anyway. Meanwhile, you'll do the right thing at every turn, while he's bribing city officials and calling in favors from friends who owe him for shady stuff."

"I think being married to him for so long has colored your worldview. I think people who are honest can do well in business, and I mean to prove it."

"Where are you going to get the funding to pay for this new startup of yours?" Mom asks.

"I'll sell my house," I say. "That should give me enough—"

"No," she says. "Don't do that." She groans. "Look, Ben, you won't think better of me for this, but I've been squirreling money away for years. I knew I couldn't trust your father, and I knew he. . .I have a quarter of a million dollars saved, and if you'll let me live with you until the divorce comes through and I have some other assets, I'll invest all of it in your company."

"I thought you said I'd fail. Dad will do whatever he can to destroy me."

"He won't have as easy a time of it with me behind you," Mom says. "And like you, I'm done rolling over and letting him dictate my life."

"I want to offer Addy a job," I say.

"Doing what? She's in public relations."

"She's brilliant," I say. "And I'm worried that, thanks to me, she may need one."

"She won't take it," Mom says.

"Even so, I'm going to offer."

"Go ahead. I'm going to call a few of the office staff that I love and see if we can't lure them over to our side as well."

"Great. I'll meet you at my place in an hour?"

"And if that little girl does take the job, tell her to put together a press release."

"Nothing nasty," I say. "I won't start this business by smearing Dad."

"You're no fun," Mom says. "But you're probably right."

I hope I am. I'm terrified Mom's initial hunch is right and this is doomed to fail. But I won't let fear stand in my way, not anymore. Never again.

12

ADDY

I'm listening to *"Another One Bites the Dust"* when Harriet stops by my cubicle. Queen always knows just what to say when I'm frustrated.

"I thought you had a meeting later?" She perches on the edge of my desk, as always.

I tug my earbuds out and sigh. "Canceled."

"Rescheduled? Or did you lose the account?"

"You make it sound like I did something wrong," I say. "The father's affair was pretty awful, and the wife is divorcing him and the son quit his job—he was my connection. It's not like his dad is going to use—"

"Did you call him? Did you pitch your ideas, at least?"

I shake my head. "He's super gross. Believe me, we do not want to work with him."

Harriet leans closer. "Do his checks bounce? Because those are the only clients we don't like—the ones who don't pay. And if they cause a lot of issues and we have to work more hours to deal with them, even better. Don't tell me he's gross. Tell me how you convinced that gross guy to sign the contract we drew up with the amazing ideas you already formulated for helping him clean up his disgusting mess."

"Harriet, I met with the uncle and the mother—there's no way that after all that—"

"Call them, right now."

"I agree." Mr. Princeton himself was apparently standing behind us.

I jump.

"Everything Harriet just said is correct, and what's more, she should not have to explain this to you. Surely you comprehend how our company works, how we remain profitable?"

I swallow.

"Why don't you call right now, and we can listen to how you handle it. I'll step in, if necessary. I looked up the Newberg Automotive chain and it's big. This is also a huge mess, which means we could generate some steady revenue from this account for a while to come."

"I won't work with the father, not if the son left. It's a bad situation. He forced his employee—"

"Didn't I just say I read up on it?" Mr. Princeton frowns. "I was unaware we allowed our account managers to pick and choose which clients were worthy of our time and attention."

My hands close around the smooth fabric of my pants suit and squeeze.

"Give me the phone," Harriet says. "I'll call him."

"No, I want her to do it," Mr. Princeton says.

I imagine it now, me calling the man who paid my father to go away and keep me from talking to his son. I contemplate calling the man who cheated on his wife *twenty* times. And if Mr. Newberg does hire me, I'd have to work with him. Have meetings with him. I think about that fact and I shudder.

Mr. Princeton folds his arms, towering over me, still

seated in my tiny plastic desk chair. "Let me put this more clearly. You're our top candidate for the promotion spot. But I can't in good conscience advance an employee who doesn't put the good of this company above all other considerations, including her personal feelings. Am I being clear?"

I nod.

He glances down at my phone and lifts his nose a bit, as if I'm a child he's nudging along.

"I can't work with him," I say. "The reason I could have gotten the account was a past relationship with the son, and the father—"

"How many of our clients are people I personally like?" Mr. Princeton asks.

Quite a few other people have gathered around—slowly at first, but now that he's speaking in such a booming voice, they're approaching faster.

No one says a word.

"I don't like any of them." He laughs. "The reason they call this work is that I'm paid to do it. Now, call him. Show me that you *get it*."

It's one of those moments in life that only come around occasionally. A crossroads in life, where the decision I make here will set me on one of two paths.

The first path is the one I would have chosen for myself last week—the road that leads to my promotion. I'm sure that, if I stroke his ego, if I tell him that his son is a fool and his wife is a moron, Mr. Newberg would hire our firm. I imagine, knowing what I know about him, that he might even get a perverse kind of pleasure out of having the woman he forcibly kept away from his son working for him to clean up this mess that separated him from his son.

Or I can take another path. I can refuse to call Benjamin, refuse to work with him, and I'll be excluded from consideration for a promotion. I might even lose my job.

Which path is the right one?

The last time I stood at a crossroads, I didn't even realize it. I was standing next to Mary in the hallway of my high school. It was the last day before summer started, and it had been five days since Ben told me he would call.

He hadn't ever called.

I saw him walking down the hall, chatting with Mike. They both looked happy—free, even. They were about to leave for college together, to attend UCLA.

I never bumped into Ben at school. The building was large and we didn't have overlapping classes or even geographic areas in our schedules. But on that day, I did see him. I almost called out his name. I almost asked him why he hadn't called.

Fear kept me from saying anything that day.

I wonder what would have happened if I had called his name. If I'd asked him why he never called. He told me just moments ago that my dad lied to me, that my dad had been paid to cover up the calls Ben made. If it's true, it means my mother was also complicit. I hadn't seen or heard from my dad in years. Mom must have mentioned Ben, and then accepted money from Dad to keep me away from him. I wish I could disbelieve all of it. I wish I could assume Ben was lying, and that neither of my parents would do something like that.

But times were hard for us then.

And this time, I know exactly where I'm standing and exactly what the decision means. I have a little more empathy for my parents than I would have back then. I've seen how hard it is to earn money. I know just how much work it takes, and how quickly things can fall apart.

But I also know what matters.

"I won't call him," I say. "And if you're a boss with integrity, if you're someone who cares about more than just dollars and cents, someone who cares about your employees and their working environment, you won't ask me again."

About half an hour later, I've gathered all my things into a box, and I'm walking out to my car. Elana didn't even try to talk to me after I got fired. Apparently I found my integrity just in time to lose everything else. When my phone rings, I almost ignore it. It's clearly not a good time, and I'm bawling so much I doubt I could talk to anyone.

But what if it's Elana? What if Harriet has gotten me a second chance? Would I call Mr. Newberg now, knowing my moral high ground cost me my job? I am panicking about how I'll make rent. I reluctantly set my box on the ground and dig my phone out of my purse.

I barely manage to hit talk in time. "Hello?"

"Addy?"

Why's Ben calling me?

"Are you there?"

I clear my voice. "I am, yeah."

"This is going to seem like it's out of left field, but I've decided to start my own business, and I know you have a great job, and I know you're amazing at it, and I know you probably don't want to leave, but I need all the good people I can get right now, so I have to at least try."

That's the longest, rambliest sentence I've ever heard anyone utter, and I'm so in love with it.

"Addy?"

"I'm here."

"Okay, well, this is my pitch. I promise to be a great boss. I promise that if you take a chance on a startup, you'll get a share of the company, and a lot of latitude in deciding what we do and how. You would have to do a lot of things you probably wouldn't need to do if you stayed at your current job, like managerial and administrative things, until I can hire someone else, but you'd also be able to set your own job description. You'd only report to me and my mom, who's helping bankroll the whole thing."

"Ben—"

"Before you turn me down, I can match your salary, I hope, and even though the benefits won't be great at first, I can reimburse you for COBRA with your current company. Eventually, I want to offer great benefits."

"Ben—"

"One more thing. This may have changed, but when we were kids, you really wanted to help people, and I hear your dad had an entrepreneurial spirit. So if any of that is still true, even if it's buried underneath the surface, consider this for a moment before turning me down."

"Ben."

"Yes. I'm listening."

"I'll take it." I'm still crying, but this time my tears are happy ones.

"Wait. You will?"

I laugh. "Half an hour ago, my boss told me I had to call and convince your dad to use our firm."

"He'd probably hire you," Ben says. "I mean, all you have to do is get him to focus on your plan and not your relationship to me. Or maybe he'd find that kind of funny. Anything he knows will upset me—"

"I flat out refused."

"Oh."

"And my boss fired me for it."

"That's awful. I wonder if you can sue for that."

"I don't need to if I have another job. A job I'm more excited about anyway." As I say the words, I realize they're true. It's not just that I've barely been making ends meet. My job has been miserable. . .because it sucked.

"This may be the first really amazing favor my dad has done for me." I can practically hear him grinning through the phone.

"I hope you still think that in two weeks, when you realize that I'm a public relations person, and that I know absolutely nothing about car repairs, and even less about startup companies."

"More than anything else, a startup needs smart people who know how to work."

"I can't really promise that I'm super smart, but I definitely know how to work." The idea of working in the same place as Ben sends a thrill through my entire body.

Until I realize that if he's my boss. . .it would be wildly inappropriate for us to date. Right? Even if he asked me out before I ever took the job. For the first time since he started his pitch, I'm a little uncomfortable about the prospect.

But then I think about my rent and my utilities and paying for my groceries. "Is it okay if I start tomorrow?"

He laughs. "We don't have an office yet, but if you're willing to work out of my house, that's great."

His house? Butterflies flutter around inside my belly. "Okay, sure."

"My mom's taking the guest bedroom, but I've got an office, a storage room we can repurpose, and a dining room. You can take your pick of whichever workspace you want. I've started putting together some preliminary task lists." He pauses. "We have a lot to do. You sure you're up for this?"

"Absolutely."

I may have chosen the wrong path ten years ago, but it feels like I'm finally back on track.

13

BEN

"Chinese water torture?" Addy asks. "Why are you researching that?"

I slam the laptop closed, my heart hammering, my hands trembling. I hope none of that is as obvious as the way she's always blushing.

"Is everything okay?" She tilts her head.

"Fine." My high, squeaky voice gives away the lie. I clear my throat and pound on my chest. "I think I may be getting a cold, but otherwise I'm fine."

"A cold?" She lifts her eyebrows. "In the middle of summer?"

Six months. It's been *six months* since Addy started working for me. Six months of inadvertent hand brushes, and long looks, and dancing the line between professional and flirty. I was looking up Chinese water torture, because I'm pretty sure it can't be as bad as what I'm dealing with right now.

The subject was restrained, their eyes covered, and then water dripped at irregular intervals on their face or body. The victim would usually begin to fear they would develop an ulcer, and even without any actual pain, they'd start to go insane.

Sign me up.

Seeing Addy every single day, but being unable to ask her out? It's worse.

Longing for Addy every single minute, and knowing I can't have her.

The worst part is that it's my *fault* I'm in this mess. I'm the one who offered her a job.

Why did I do that?

She's brilliant. Far smarter than I even realized. She's also competent. She's fast, and helpful, and friendly, and kind. I'm not sure we would have lasted six months without her. I could start counting the ways she's saved this new enterprise, but I'd start losing track around a dozen, I'm sure.

I recognized some of the things that made her amazing when I was eighteen. I really did. I knew she was different—better—than any of the other girls I'd met. But either she's grown to be even more spectacular, or I didn't have the depth yet to realize *how much* better she was than every other girl I knew. Either way, Addy's everything I ever wanted and then some.

And she's just out of reach. Because I'm an idiot.

"I came over to talk to you about the Enterprise account. They wanted to know if you're positive we can handle the volume."

"Of course we can." I lean back in my chair. "Did you send them the projections we prepared?"

She points at my laptop. "I sent them to you to review last night. As soon as you approve the figures, I will."

Right. Of course.

"But apparently you have some pressing research to do?" Her lips twitch a little bit. I've discovered there are only two reasons for that—suppressed humor about something she thinks might be rude, which is what I'm dealing with right now, or else she's heard some noise that annoys her.

"If you're done making fun of me, I'll pull up those projections and review them."

"Try to let the tiny things go," she says. "Attention to detail is good. But picking over every single tiny thing the client won't even notice—"

"Is obsessive," Mom says. "I've told him that before."

I hate when they gang up on me. "Attention to detail is one of the reasons we haven't had more issues than we have."

"Yes, you're fabulous," Addy says.

"You're the very best CEO in the world." Mom beams at me.

And now I feel, somehow, more annoyed than if they'd disagreed with me. I scowl as I open the laptop. As expected, the numbers look great. I may be the one they're hassling, but Addy has at least as much attention to detail as I do.

"Do you think we're likely to land the account?" I'm trying not to get my hopes up. But with the signing bonus, we could prep to open the third location I've been planning, before my dad will even realize it's a perfect spot.

"I think it's a lock," Addy says.

Having her take over the new account presentations was a stroke of genius. Her PR background has taught her to handle people easily: how to read them, how to manipulate them (as bad as that sounds), and how to win them over. Her looks don't hurt on that front either. "Garett had nothing but glowing comments about you."

Everyone does.

"I wanted to remind you that I have an interview

tomorrow," she says. "At HotHead PR. Remember? I won't be here all afternoon, if things go well."

Half of me is desperately hoping she won't get the job. I know the only reason she came to work with me was that she lost her job thanks to her unswerving loyalty, but she has been phenomenal. I have no idea how we'll replace her.

On the other hand, I've wanted to ask her out for six months. Actually, six months and a week, since the day she popped up like a daisy in that hideous press conference, putting all those reporters in their place. Some people might have just asked her out—it's not like we're a huge company with lots of rules. But those people don't have Benjamin Newberg as a father, the predator who's always asking out his employees.

Every time I thought about inviting her to dinner, every time I wanted to take her hand with my own, I'd think about my dad. What he would do. How he would *take* what he wanted, no matter how uncomfortable she might be saying no.

And I would sprint the other direction, figuratively at least.

I've also been doing a lot of actual running each morning. More than I did in high school, even. So much running. I've never been in better shape. Apparently pent-up energy is great for encouraging exercise.

"I thought you said you couldn't bear the thought of leaving us," Mom says.

"I do love working here," Addy says, "but I'm a public relations specialist. You can find someone else who'll do a much better job running the office and securing new accounts. I've been muddling through, and I appreciate your patience, but trust me. It'll be better for everyone if I'm not working here in a few weeks."

Could she possibly want to leave so I can ask her out,

or is she dying to get away from me? Have I done a worse job covering up my feelings than I thought?

"Come on, Ben, say something. Keep her here. Offer her more money."

"I'll miss her," I say. "I'll miss her a *lot*, but I think she's right. A public relations job, especially as an account executive, would be a much better position for her. It sounds like the people at HotHead really get how valuable she is."

Mom throws her arms up in the air.

The phone rings, and Mom and Addy both dive to answer it.

"It's for you," Addy says, handing the receiver to Mom.

We're in an office now, albeit a small one, but we don't have separate rooms yet. We all share one big workspace, saving the separate areas for a break room and a conference room. When someone's on a call, we try to be quiet, at least until we know who's calling. The call isn't very long.

Mom hangs up, stands up, and leaps into the air, pumping her fist up and down. "It's final! It's *final!*"

"Whoa, it is?" Addy's beaming.

Heck, I'm beaming too.

"The lawyer's sending the signed decree over, and guess what?" Mom's eyes are so bright.

"What?"

"The request for appeal was denied." Mom's smile is so big it nearly splits her face in half. "It's *final* and it wasn't overturned."

Which means. . .that we own Dad's company now. I can hardly contemplate the magnitude of what just happened. When the court awarded Mom full ownership of Newberg Auto, we were all floored. Of course, in Georgia, it's up to the judge's discretion how to split things.

Dad has several other businesses, all of which are doing quite well. My parents also own a few homes, including a beach house in Miami, a cabin in Colorado, and a villa in Mexico.

But the judge decided to split Dad's ownership in all the small businesses *and* award the biggest one entirely to Mom. He also gave Mom the Miami beach house, but told Dad that by giving him the villa and the cabin, he was treated equitably for Mom taking the entire marital share of Newberg Automotive. Dad's eyes bulged out, his skin turning nearly purple, and then he charged toward us. The court's security personnel had to restrain him.

Our lawyer told us the appellate court would reapportion it for sure.

Only, apparently they didn't.

"What will you do?" Addy asks. "Will you keep running both?"

"Your uncle's share still belongs to Dad," Mom says.

"That's a real shame," I say.

"I think he might trade my partial share in the other businesses for that interest," Mom says. "I doubt he wants anything to do with us, either."

"Or maybe he'll hang on to be spiteful," Addy says.

"I doubt it. He'll think of his own defeat every time we interact," Mom says. "He'll believe we'll run it into the ground without him running things, which makes retaining it a bad investment. If we do manage to run it well, he'll hate that even worse."

"You're right. If you offer to make that trade and he takes it, I vote that we just merge both companies."

Mom's smile is radiant—the smile I remember her making at my spelling bee as a kid. The smile she made when a friendly robin landed on her arm at the park, once. The smile she makes whenever she witnesses me and Addy flirting.

"I'll call him right now," Mom says.

"Don't," I say. "Let's celebrate today."

But she's already dialing, and before I can stop her, I can hear my dad's voice bellowing in her ear. It's more like a squeak to me, but I know how it sounds to her.

"No, Benjamin, that's not why I'm calling. Gloating is your thing, not mine. I was calling to propose a trade."

There's a pause. Dad cannot let anything go without saying his piece.

"Sure, I suppose. But the reason I'm calling is to offer to trade my partial ownership in Underhill, in Quickie, and in Portable. I'll trade you my forty percent share in all three companies for Chris' forty percent in Newberg Auto."

The line goes entirely silent.

When he finally does speak, it's brief. When my mom hangs up, she looks a little dazed.

"What?" Addy asks. "What did he say?"

"He laughed," she says. "Apparently the partial interests are worth twenty percent more than the share in Newberg."

I shrug. "Who cares?"

"He needs a reason to feel like he's getting something over on me," Mom says. "And I'm fine with it. So he's having his lawyer draw up those documents now. He thinks we can get it as a modification to the decree, but it would be a mutual change to the decree terms. We're still officially divorced as of today."

A tightness I didn't realize was constricting my chest eases. It's not *my* divorce, but Mom's unhappiness has hung over my head my entire life.

And it's finally gone.

I look at the calendar for today—nothing at all planned, and we worked right through lunch like usual. "Why don't we knock off work early and have a late lunch somewhere fancy to celebrate?" I ask. "We don't have anything else we *have* to do today."

Before Mom or Addy can answer, the phone rings again. We don't usually get quite so many calls. We may have to hire a receptionist soon—except we probably won't need to if we merge with the main office.

Wow, that's a lot of changes in a very short period of time.

"It's a great morning at Vivian Auto," Addy says.

We've been operating under a business in Mom's name for months, but it still sounds strange to me. I wonder whether Mom will want to collapse into Newberg, or change its name as well.

"Oh, well, maybe. Do you mind holding for a moment so I can ask?" She covers the receiver.

"What's up?" I ask.

"It's the PR company," she whispers. "The president's going out of town tomorrow morning unexpectedly. They want to move my interview to today—like, right now, basically."

So much for celebrating. "Uh, sure, that's fine." It's not like I can tell her we have too much planned. Geez. I know that I want her to take the job, but now that she's going for the interview, it feels too real. I wonder how much of my failure to ask her out had to do with my fear she'd say no, or that if we dated, it wouldn't work out.

I've been blaming my fear of becoming like my dad, but maybe Addy means too much for me to risk ruining it.

The thought of not seeing her every day makes me want to curl up and cry like a little baby. I bet she'd think that was super hot. Sheesh. Moments later, she's waving bye and ducking out the door.

"You're an idiot." Mom sinks into one of the wingback chairs in front of my desk.

"What?"

"You, my darling, gorgeous, brilliant, kind son, are an idiot. Of the highest order."

"Did you already start drinking?" I look around for glasses.

She snorts, which isn't very ladylike. "That girl is head over heels for you."

I practically choke.

"And you're almost shoving her out the door. What on earth are you thinking?"

"Shoving her?" I point at the door. "She raced out of here."

She stands up. "Let's go get that drink you talked about."

"Drink?" My voice cracks again. Could I be going through a second puberty? "I mentioned *lunch*."

"Oh. Maybe I'm the one who was thinking of a drink. Regardless, let's go."

Three hours later, Mom's still pounding margaritas. She's still calling me an idiot, too, but she's not doing it quite as forcefully. "You need to ask her out—no, wait. Just plant one on her."

"Tell me how that's any different than something Dad would do."

She holds up two fingers. "For one, you're not married. And she isn't either." She looks at her fingers closely.

"Do you mean, first, neither of us are married?"

"That's what I said." Mom frowns. "And third and foremost, she *wants* you to kiss her. I've seen her stare after you largingly."

"*Longingly?*"

"Duh." She presses her hand against the table. "You're not making a lot of sense."

She did just end a marriage of more than thirty years.

I should cut her some slack. "Right. I should call you a cab."

"Is that your way of saying I need to go home?" Her eyebrows waggle.

I suppress a laugh. "I'm more suggesting it."

"Fine." She scowls. "Fine. Fine. I'm fine. Fine."

I leave some money on the table next to her practically uneaten fajitas and take her arm. Luckily there are loads of cabs in this area, and it doesn't take me long to hail one. "Are you sure you can get inside, once the cab gets you to my place?"

Her eye roll is epic. "I used to change your diapers. Change your diapers!"

I'm walking to my car when my phone rings. And it's Addy. I swipe so fast and so hard I nearly drop my phone. "Hello?"

"They offered me a job!" She sounds ecstatic.

My heart falls into my loafers. "That's great." Turns out, I'm not amazing at faking it. Even to me, my response sounds more like Eeyore than Richard Simmons.

"Are you alright?"

"Oh, I'm fine," I say, "totally fine."

"Are you sure?"

"Did you already tell them yes?"

She pauses. "I mean, you're about to merge, right? Then you *really* won't need me."

"Where are you?"

"I'm downtown," she says. "Their office is *amazing*."

"I can meet you. We could talk about it over dinner."

We've gotten takeout when we worked late. We've even had lunch with my mom a few times, but in the six months we've been working together, I've been very careful never to ask her to eat with me alone. Every time

I think about our flirty lunch at the Korean place, my heart accelerates.

"Dinner?"

"I'm asking you on a date," I say. "In case that wasn't clear."

"Oh."

Mom's right. I'm an idiot. Why didn't I wait for her to take the job before doing this? Because I need to know whether, if she takes it, I'll ever see her again. If she turns me down for this date, I'll offer her twice her salary just to keep her in my life. I'd have to live on a pittance if we don't merge, but who cares?

Oh my gosh, I am my father.

"Yes," she says. "I'd love to go to dinner with you."

It feels like I'm soaring, sailing, no, flying through the air. "How about Little Bear?"

"That's my favorite restaurant!"

She says that like I didn't already know. I filed it away months ago when Mary mentioned it. "Perfect."

"I can be there in twenty minutes and get us on the waitlist. Are you okay with a long wait?"

If she's by my side, sure. But I've found that the host or hostess usually gets me in much faster with a generous tip. "I'm game."

Twenty minutes and a substantial bribe for the hostess later, our table's ready. I'm as jittery as I was before prom, waiting for Addy to show. I think about her dress that night, and her smile. I think about how we had milkshakes and talked for. . .not nearly long enough.

"Ben!"

I pivot on my heel, and even though she's wearing the same thing she had on earlier, her outfit hits me like a right hook to the jaw. Delicate pink business shirt. Dark suit coat and matching fitted pants. Somehow both feminine and professional. Put together, capable, and still somehow jaw-droppingly beautiful.

Don't mess this up, Ben. Do not *mess this up.*

I smile back at her, and the hostess waves for us to follow her.

"Wait." Addy pauses. "Where's your mom? Shouldn't she be celebrating? You didn't ditch her, did you?"

My lip curls up. "She over-celebrated already. She's in a timeout."

Addy snickers. "You're kidding."

"I'm definitely not. I sent her home."

"You're such a cute son." She tilts her head. "I'm so happy for her." She's a little careless in how she's walking, swinging her arms.

When she gets a little too close to me, I seize the moment and snag her hand, interlacing our fingers. She stiffens for one split second before tightening her fingers on mine. Her half smile tells me she's not just putting up with me—she's happy too.

"Wall or aisle?" I ask.

Addy takes the aisle, leaving me a view of the whole room. She must remember me saying I spend half the meal turned around when I'm sitting with my back to everyone else. "Thanks."

She shrugs. "I'm no Jason Bourne. I'm fine seeing no one around me, as long as I can see you." And then she blushes.

I love it so much.

"Why'd you ask me to dinner?"

I'm an idiot. I'm a moron. I'm too afraid.

Mom's words roll around in my brain. She has another job. She can leave and never see me again if she wants. I'm not being a predator.

I'm seizing the moment.

I'm living in the now.

"I like you," I say. "You're beautiful, you're funny, you're smart. The idea of not seeing you at work every day." I press my fist to my chest. "It makes me hurt right here."

She blinks. "Are you saying I shouldn't have taken the job?"

"I don't know what the future holds," I say. "But I know that I want you."

She opens her mouth and then closes it again.

"If you like working with me, then I want that. If having your own space will make you happier to see me after work, then I want that. I want you any way I can get you, at work or at home. The more the better."

A tear rolls down her cheek.

Oh, no. What have I done?

I want to lean across the table and wipe it away, but alarm bells are sounding in my head. She's *crying*. Does that mean I *am* my dad? How can I take it back? "Addy, I'm sorry."

She shakes her head. "Don't be sorry." She swipes at the tear. "I cry when I'm really, ridiculously happy. It's a whole thing."

What's she saying?

"I love you, Ben." She laughs then, a high, clear, sweet sound, not at all shrill. "I should not be saying that right now, probably. I mean, we've never even kissed, not as adults anyway."

That's a problem I can solve. That's a puzzle I can work. I circle the table just as our waiter walks up. "No tip unless you walk away."

His eyes widen and he turns around and practically runs.

"What were you saying?" I reach for her shoulders and tug her to her feet.

She swallows hard, her eyes on my mouth.

My fingers delicately trace her cheek, the line of her jaw, and then tilt her head upward, toward me. And I lean down, down, down, not rushing, not this. Not the most important kiss of my entire life—our second first kiss. I stop a hair away from her mouth, her breath mingling with mine. "I love you too," I say. And then I press my mouth to hers.

The world drops away.

The restaurant.

The job situation.

My address.

There's only Addy and me, me and Addy, her mouth on mine, her arms sliding around my waist. Those are the only things that matter in the whole entire world.

She loves me.

We can work out the rest.

14

ADDY

Some days, I wish I'd never taken this job.

Hudson, the CEO of HotHead, is manic, no lie. He works and works and works and works, and when he's working, he expects everyone to work.

But he would never dream of asking me to take a case I didn't feel comfortable handling, and he'd never put money ahead of people. I'm also learning a lot about my job that I didn't learn in school, and I didn't learn at Princeton PR either. Hudson didn't tell a single lie during the interview. He told me working here would be brutal, but that it would be worth it. It is, both.

"You're finally off?" Ben asks the second he picks up.

"Finally," I say. "But you'll never believe what I got to do."

Ben listens, patiently, every single day, at least feigning interest in the public relations stuff that I gush about. But this time, he'll actually be excited. "I met Cliff Owens."

Silence. Did I lose him?

"Did you hear me?"

"*The* Cliff Owens?"

Ben loves cars—hardly surprising for someone who

owns a car repair company. But his second love is baseball, and Cliff Owens is the Braves' best shot at winning the World Series this time around. "The one and only."

"There are probably lots of guys named Cliff Owens," he says.

"But this is the one you're thinking of, Atlanta Braves player, Cliff Owens."

"Please, please, please tell me that he hasn't done something awful."

"Not him," I say, "but his girlfriend."

"His girlfriend?"

"I think it's probably his ex, now," I say. "Apparently she was selling prescription drugs to all the players' significant others."

"But there's no punishment for him, right?"

I should hope not. "I am quite good at my job," I say. "He did nothing wrong, and in fact, didn't even know about it. I promise, no one will hear anything different."

"I really do love you," he says. "And now, you're protecting the hopes and dreams of millions."

I laugh.

"Are we still on for dinner?"

"Sure," I say. "I'm just getting to my car." Except, when I exit the elevator for the parking garage and cross the lot, my car's not there. "Uh, this is nerve-wracking. My car is gone. Tell me you know something about that."

"You said you were a month overdue on your oil change." He says it the same way I might say, *the house is on fire*.

"Honey, a *lot* of people get oil changes a month late. The world keeps on turning."

"I'm not letting my girlfriend die in a fiery crash that could have been prevented. I'm on the ground level. I'll be down to you in two minutes."

I can't quite help my smile. I should never have told

him in the first place. Fiery crash, indeed. When his big black truck pulls up alongside me, the newer version of what he drove in high school, my smile only widens.

He rolls down the window and whistles. "Hey, baby. Need a ride?"

Sometimes it still hits me, his beauty, and how far out of my league he is. "Sure," I say. "That would be great. But only if you're going to stop for food. Otherwise, I might eat your armrests."

"These?" After I climb in, he shifts his armrest up and down. "They're made of rubber. We can do better."

"Little Bear, right?"

He sighs. "They said they lost our reservation, but that's okay. I have another idea."

"Uh, I called and made that reservation myself." I whip out my phone. I'm going to give that hostess a piece of my mind.

Ben's hand captures mine. "Let's not get all agitated and twirly today. Not on Cliff Owens day."

"Oh, that reminds me." I pull my purse up on my lap and rummage around in it while Ben pulls out of the parking garage. "I got you something." I finally find it, the surface smooth, the laces pristine. "Look."

"I can't look—I'm driving." But when the light ahead of us turns red, he cranes his neck. "What. Is. That?"

"It's just what you think it is." I toss it to him.

He gasps and fumbles it. It lands on the floorboard with a thunk just as the light turns green. He swears under his breath as he kicks it, and I lean over and snag it again. "Why would you throw it!? A ball autographed by Cliff Owens!"

"Honey, I'm going to see him a few more times. I've already ordered a dozen balls on Amazon. You're going to have as many autographed balls as you want."

"Only a dozen?" His eyebrows go up.

I exhale. "Fine. I'll order another *two* dozen."

He beams. "That's my girl."

And I am. His, I mean.

It still feels surreal sometimes. I'm not the kind of girl who gets the best-looking guy in Atlanta. A guy who's now worth tens of millions of dollars. A man who oversees hundreds of other people. A man whose smile makes my pulse pound. A man whom other women whip around to check out.

I'm the plain girl. The one who wears moon boots. The one whose dad ruins things and whose mom means well but botches stuff, too. But he's here, picking me up because he took my car to get the oil changed. He's smiling at *me*. This is my life, now.

I daydream so long that when the truck stops, I'm almost disoriented. "Where are we?"

"If Little Bear's slammed, I figured this is the next best place."

"IHOP?" I can't keep the incredulity out of my voice.

"Not just any IHOP." He circles the car and opens my door. "*The* IHOP where we had shakes after ditching prom. The place where we chatted for hours after our first kiss."

The memory of that night, that perfect, bizarre, unlikely night, hits me like cold water to the face. Why is he bringing me here now? "You're what? Desperate for a milkshake?"

He laughs. "Something like that."

As we walk to the entrance, I notice that there are hardly any cars in the lot. It's a weekend, and IHOP may not be Little Bear, but it should be fairly busy. Why isn't anyone here? We're met at the front by a hostess and two other people.

"Welcome to IHOP, Miss Thorley." The hostess curtsies.

Why's the hostess curtsying?

"Addy, you're going to notice as soon as we walk inside that no one else is here. I rented the restaurant for the night."

Why would he do that?

"Because that night we came here, it felt like the whole world fell away. It felt like the only people who mattered were you and I. No one had ever made me feel that way before, and no one has since."

I don't know what to say, so I follow him through the door. He's right—no other patrons sit inside. The entire dining room is totally clear. Except for a pair of moon boots sitting in the middle of one of the tables, with a big red bow on them.

"What's going on?" I stop, resisting the pull of his tugging hand. "Ben Newberg, tell me right now."

"Just roll with it, Addison Thorley," he says with an exasperated smile, "for once in your life."

I am not a person who rolls. I'm a person who accelerates or brakes. I never roll. But for his sake, I'll try.

He drags me toward the table. On either side of the boots is a shake. One chocolate and one strawberry.

"We should have eaten something that night," I grumble.

He laughs. "Let me say my piece and then you can order anything you want."

"Perfect."

"Addy Thorley, you've always been the girl of my dreams. It took me a while to see it—too long. You walk your own walk on earth or the moon, you clomp down any trail unafraid, and you're always the first to blaze your own path."

"How many boot references do you think you can make tonight?"

He laughs. "I'm not sure yet."

I roll my eyes, but he knows I'm not mad. How could I be?

"Now, for this next part, I need you to put these on." He tosses the red bow to the side and hands me my boots.

"Where did you even get these?"

"It took three hours," he says. "Your mom and I almost gave up."

One boot has some fluff coming out of the back.

"Something might have tried to make a nest in that one." He scrunches his nose.

I very nearly drop them.

"But don't worry. They're totally clean, and there's nothing in either one."

I sigh. "Why do you want me to put them on?"

He holds out his phone. "Humor me."

I groan. "Fine." I slide out of my pumps, and slip my foot into the non-rodent-chewed one first. And then, reluctantly, I push my left foot into the one with the fuzzy spot. Except it can't go very far—something's stuffed inside the boot. I scream and drop the shoe, stumbling backward.

Ben catches me, his face far too pleased.

"What's going on?"

"Do you really think I would bring a boot with a mouse in it?" He shakes his head. "Did it feel furry or squishy?"

Now that he mentions it, whatever was inside that boot was hard and pointy. Like a box. A small, square box. *For the love.* I shove away from Ben and snatch the boot again, jamming my hand down inside it. The box I pull out is bright blue.

It says *Tiffany's* on top.

Something clogs up inside my chest as I hold it in my

hands, and when I turn back toward Ben, he's kneeling, his hands clasped in front of him like he's praying.

"Marry me, Addy. Please?"

"You're supposed to be on one knee," I hiss. "You're doing it wrong."

"No." He shakes his head. "When you're really worried about something, when it's all that matters to you, one knee isn't enough. I swear that if you say yes, I will spend the rest of my life making up for the ten years I let go to waste. I'll do anything it takes to make you happy. I'll care for you and only you. And I will never, ever let anything or anyone come between us again."

I toss the box on the table and drag Ben to his feet. "Of course I'll marry you, idiot. Now, kiss me."

And he does. Oh, he does.

"You're saying he dumped you. . .when you told him you didn't want to have kids?" I shake my head. It makes no sense. "You've always said you didn't want children."

Tears stream down Mary's face. "I told him that on our first date."

"I remember," I say. "I was there."

"Right." Mary's holding her engagement ring between her thumb and her forefinger, staring at it numbly.

It breaks my heart to see her like this. In all the world, other than my sweet husband and two darling little girls, there's no one I love more than her. I don't want to hurt her worse—that's the last thing I want to do—but I have to know. "Can I ask you something?"

Mary's still staring, and her eyes look almost glassy.

"Mary."

She jolts, like she just heard me for the first time.

"Can I ask you something?"

"Didn't you just? I mean, that question is still a question."

Her droll sense of humor is actually reassuring. It's 110

percent Mary. "Right. But that usually implies that I have something more important to ask. Something I'm worried might upset you."

Mary drops the ring onto my coffee table and claws her way back onto my sofa. "How much worse can today really get? Ask away."

"Why don't you want kids?"

Mary blinks. "Are you serious?"

"No, I mean, I know *why*. Your parents were awful, yes. Your mom left, and your dad was a drunk, and you had to raise Trudy and yourself." I shrug. "It's not fair, but it's kind of what made you this awesome person that you are."

"I don't understand."

"You love my girls. I've seen you with them. They love you, too, and you're not miserable when you're with them."

Mary closes her eyes, and I could sew my own mouth shut. Why today, of all days, am I pressing her on this?

But I know why.

Foster was perfect for her. He was charitable, polished, handsome, and even wealthy—probably Atlanta's most eligible bachelor, at least since Ben went off the market. I was over the moon for Mary when they started dating, and when he proposed? I would never admit it, but I already bought her the cutest little dress in a size three months.

And a pair of booties.

And a blanket.

She *has* always said she didn't want kids, but I didn't really *believe* she meant it. Apparently Foster didn't believe her either. Not until today, anyway.

"He's like Foster Fancy Pants the fifth or something. You had to know his family would want you to have children."

Mary swallows, her eyes staring at the wall. At least she's not still clasping the dumb ring.

"Look, I don't mean to pry, I really don't, but you seem pretty shaken up. I want to make sure that you've really thought this through. That boy seems to be head over heels for you—"

She shakes her head. "When he realized I wasn't kidding, he didn't even hesitate." She finally turns toward me, her eyes haunted. "He pressed and pushed and insisted, but once he saw I meant what I said. . ." She shrugs. "That was it. It was like the two weeks we spent planning the wedding, the lunch we had with his mother, the invitations we picked out, none of it mattered. If I wasn't going to pop out children for him, then we were through."

I wonder, for the first time, whether this has less to do with what Mary *thinks* she doesn't want, and more to do with Mary's own view of her value as a person. Also, I'm revising my assessment of Foster. If he doesn't love my Mary enough to stand by her *no matter what*, then he doesn't deserve her.

My dearest friend is going to have children—I'm not sure how I know it, I just do. But before she can possibly fathom caring for a child, she has to realize that she's worthy of love herself. She needs to know in her bones that she's lovable in a way her family never taught her she was.

Foster failed just as miserably as they did.

Which means, no matter how eligible, he's not the right man for her.

The right man for Mary will see the shining light inside of her.

He won't balk when she protests that she doesn't want children.

He won't care if she says she's married to her job.

He won't mind that she doesn't have faith in herself yet.

Because he'll stand beside her until she finds it.

I just wish she'd hurry up and find him. Watching her like this is like watching a wrecking ball take out the Taj Mahal. Or watching a dog eat a perfect wedding cake while no one's looking. Or watching my beautiful babies drool all over a fresh, crisp paperback book.

It's a travesty, that's what it is.

Unfortunately, there's not much I can do. Mary won't listen to me. She won't *hear* me when I tell her that I know she can balance work and family in a way her parents never did. She won't *comprehend* when I tell her that she's nothing like her mother or her father. She won't *understand* when I tell her that the greatest joy in life comes from serving someone else and forgetting yourself.

But one day, hopefully soon, she'll experience it all. And when she does? It will be glorious.

"Alright, listen." I plop down next to her on the sofa and throw an arm around her shoulders. "You are brilliant. You are kind. You are talented. You are loyal." I sigh. "And Foster is a misguided, moronic, selfish pig. You're lucky to be free of him so you can spend more time with me and your sister, Trudy, whom I think might really need your help right now."

Mary wipes her cheeks and shakes her head and lets go of her misery, like she always does. In all the years I've known her, the only thing that has ever pulled Mary out of a good wallow is helping someone else. It's exactly what will make her the world's best mother, once she realizes that's what she was born to be.

"Thank you, Addy. I love you."

"I love you too, Mary. Always have."

"I'm lucky to have you."

"You really are," I say. "Now, let's figure out what awful

things we're going to do to Foster to make him pay for being such a fool."

Mary laughs like I'm kidding. If she only knew. Ben's mom was just talking about this awful daughter of one of her friends—a gold digger who only cares about marrying someone with a fat bank account. Someone just like Foster. Wouldn't he just deserve someone like Jessica Hansen? Wasn't that her name?

Nah. That's too good for him. I'll have to think of something worse.

"I want ice cream," Mary says.

"Hey," I say. "That's great."

"What's great?"

"That we've already graduated to eating our feelings! I'm so proud of you!" Laxative in his ice cream? The idea has merit, but I'm not sure how I'd carry it out. It may take me days, weeks even, to think of the perfect revenge, but unlike Mary, I'm patient enough to find it, and I never forget a grudge.

He'll get what's coming to him for making Mary feel this way.

"Double chocolate fudge?" Mary smiles. "What can't that fix?"

"Not much," I say. "Not much at all."

The good news is that you can't keep a shining light like Mary down for very long. I see bright things in her future.

⚜

Due to LENGTH LIMITATIONS of the Sweet and Swoony romance promo, I wasn't able to include a chapter showing Ben and Addy's wedding. BUT IF YOU WANT IT, DON'T WORRY!!

If you've already signed up for my newsletter, you've

already gotten an invite to download the wedding bonus chapter! It's zany. It's a mess. And it's also beautiful. (The story doesn't NEED it, but I had fun writing it!)

If you haven't joined my newsletter yet and you WANT the bonus chapter, you can sign up for it here and get the bonus chapter immediately: https://dl.bookfunnel.com/ttwkpfm842.

**And if you'd like to read about Mary's story (FOR FREE!), you can grab it right now! Finding Faith is currently FREE on all platforms. If you keep scrolling, you can even read the first chapter of Finding Faith to see whether you'l like it. (Hint, it's Mary, Addy's best friend from Finding Grace, getting her happily ever after!)

B. E. BAKER
Finding
Faith
a novel

15

FINDING FAITH SAMPLE CHAPTER

By the time my friends turned seven, not a single one of them actually believed in Santa.

Ironically, that's the year my faith in the big guy began.

I was skeptical from the start. A fat, bearded man shoots down chimneys or climbs through windows to deliver presents to lots of kids he doesn't even know? He travels via a sleigh that's powered by flying deer?

Yeah, right.

I always gravitated toward science and math, because their clear-cut answers helped make sense of the world. I learned about Occam's Razor while preparing my science fair project in second grade. It dictates that all other things being equal, the simplest explanation is probably the correct one. That's why, the Christmas after I turned seven, when all my friends were catching up to what I'd known all along, that Santa's a big, fat, phony, I began to believe.

After all, that year I woke up to a decorated tree with blinking lights, and a whole truckload of fancy, beautifully wrapped presents. My options to explain this baffling event were: 1) a red-suited man who lives in the North Pole brought me toys in a magical sack; or 2) my dad actually saved some of the money he would otherwise spend on beer to buy the presents for me as a surprise. I could count on one hand the number of times Dad left the house, if I excluded walking around the corner to the auto-repair place where he worked, or walking to the convenience store for more alcohol.

In fact, if I hadn't learned to steal tiny amounts of cash from my dad's paycheck stash, my little sister Gertrude and I wouldn't have even had hotdogs and ramen to eat. Trudy and I still twitch every time we pass a hotdog stand.

It was clear, given what I knew, that Santa must exist.

I stand up, and clear my throat. Almost a hundred sets of eyes turn toward me, and the thrill I feel every year when Sub-for-Santa season commences fills my chest. Large nutcrackers stand guard by the door, and faux holly garland drapes along every surface. A sparkly, rainbow lit tree covered in ornaments we've been given by grateful parents as thank yous over the years decorates the conference room. It looks cheerier than usual, but it's still essentially one big table with a podium up front, and a hundred folding metal chairs in rows toward the back.

"Welcome to the organizational meeting for this year's Sub-for-Santa program, sponsored locally by the United Way. I'm delighted you're all here. We can't wait to work with you to bring a little wonder to a lot of children who haven't had enough of that in their lives. My name is Mary Wiggin, and I'm the President of the Sub-for-Santa program here in Atlanta."

Smiles sprout on the faces of volunteers all around me, which is more impressive given the fact that they're all sitting on hard, metal chairs.

I continue. "We are here to uplift the lives of as many

kids as we possibly can. I'm proud to say that this program has grown consistently each of the eight years that I've been in charge, and I hope to be able to say the same next year."

Everyone claps and I wait for them to finish.

"Many of you are familiar, and I'm so pleased to see you returning year after year. Do any of you repeat sponsors recall the number one rule?"

Three hands shoot up. I point at a lady in a bright pink sweater sporting a reindeer wearing magenta lipstick.

"Only nominate families who are super poor?" she asks.

I nod my head. "We do want to ensure the families placed on our list are in need, mostly because our resources are limited and we want to help as many people as we can, but it's not our number one rule. Anyone else remember that?"

Now that one of them was wrong, they're all nervous about answering. Only one hand stays raised, the green polished fingers waving wildly, like a kid waving down an ice cream truck. "Yes, Paisley?"

My perky secretary from work is helping me run the program for the third year in a row. She's paid for some of her time, but at minimum wage. Ironically, she doesn't seem to care about anything at our real job where she's paid far, far more, but she's my most enthusiastic volunteer with Sub-for-Santa. Paisley's just made for Christmas, I guess.

She beams. "Don't ruin the magic."

"Exactly, yes, that's rule number one. We do not want any of these children, not a single one, to know where these presents really originate. The reason this program works is that these kids believe in the cultural fiction that a jolly fat man with a loving, hardworking wife supervises a host of tiny elves. The kids need to believe that someone has noticed the kind things, the good things, and the right things they've done this year. They need to believe that someone cares about them. If they think these presents stem from pity, how will they feel instead?"

Paisley's hand shoots up again, and she bounces up and down in her chair. I suppress my grin and call on the heavy-set man sporting a full beard with his arm raised behind her.

"But isn't that kind of a lie?" he asks. "I mean, eventually they'll figure it out, and they'll either be mad or feel like idiots."

I frown. I should never have trusted a man with howling wolves on his t-shirt.

"Were you ever a recipient of Christmas gifts, something like the Sub-for-Santa program?" I ask.

He shakes his head. "Nah, my parents didn't need handouts."

I grit my teeth. "As someone who was a recipient, trust me. They won't be angry when they find out people cared enough to keep their donation a secret."

"You're only one person. You don't know how everyone will feel."

Note to self: install ejection seats before next year's opening meeting.

"I can't speak for everyone," I say, "but neither can you. Respectfully, speaking from ten years of experience with this program, I think you're wrong. I've seen a lot of reactions and heard from a lot of children. I've heard from kids who were participants year after year on both sides. Many of them are involved to this day, just like me. We aren't lying to these children, and anyone who believes that Sub-for-Santa is perpetuating a lie should leave."

I pause and glance meaningfully toward the back

door. No one stands up. "If you're all staying, I'd love to share something with you that might help you understand how this will work. When I was younger, my mom left our family. My sister was not quite four years old. After Mom left, our dad started drinking heavily. Now I have a label for what he was: a poorly functioning alcoholic. Those were difficult times in the Wiggin household."

Paisley gives me two thumbs up and I want to stop this presentation to hug her.

"That Christmas I was old enough to know that Santa wasn't real. He was a lie, and I knew we'd wake up Christmas morning the same as every other morning. I'd make ramen for my sister, and we'd pretend it wasn't the crappiest day of the year."

I make eye contact with a dozen people, making sure they're all listening.

"Except that's not what happened. For the first time in a very long time, something great happened to us. Santa Claus was real, and he brought us a beautiful tree with multitudes of presents underneath it. Once a year, I knew that even if my parents thought I was worthless, someone somewhere cared. When I did finally discover that it wasn't Santa, but in fact a group of extraordinary people who wanted me to have a fantastic day, that meant more to me than the fiction of Santa."

A tear springs to my eye, as it always does this time of year when I think back to that first Christmas. I wipe it away.

"Sub-for-Santa," I say, "is a program that allows good people to give to those who need love, for no benefit to themselves. We should be doing things like this all year, but that's too tall an order, so we settle for one day a year of selfless service and love to children who will truly appreciate the gesture. The real reason we never, ever, let the children know where the presents come from is that—"

Paisley's waving so frantically I'm worried she's going to poke the guy next to her in the eye. A lawsuit would eat up all our funds and the program would collapse. I sigh, but the corners of my mouth turn up a little anyway.

"Yes, Pais?"

"If the kids figure out it's coming from a charity, they'll feel patronized. We want them to feel like someone values them, like they're worthwhile, not like they're getting presents out of pity or guilt. Eventually, they'll be old enough to realize that there may be a real Santa somewhere, but he can't really reach everyone, so other people help out and do some of his work for him."

There may be a real Santa somewhere? I can't help but smile, because other than her small delusion, she's spot on. If she exhibited half this much zeal in the tax office where we both work, she wouldn't still be my secretary. She'd have been promoted to office manager.

"Well said Paisley, thank you. If these children believe in Santa, they also believe that they matter to someone. If these children know rich people are donating things to poor kids who aren't loved, they'll feel lesser. That's obviously the opposite of our goal."

As I work my way through the rest of the rules, my heart lifts and it finally starts to feel like the holiday season is upon us. Eventually, it's time to pass out nomination forms and sponsor requirements.

"I have a list of volunteers that we've collected from several church groups and businesses, as well as employees, friends and neighbors. You're all here because you offered to sponsor a family, or be part of my core team to help administer the entire operation, or both. I appreciate that greatly. We still have one more week to collect volunteers and then I'll finalize the nominations for participants. Please write down the information on anyone you have now, and bring it to me. The sooner we have nominations, the sooner we can contact them for permission, and request the documentation we need to ensure our efforts go to the right place. Last year, we helped five hundred and thirty-two families, with more than eleven hundred children. My goal for this year is to reach six hundred families and fifteen hundred children. If you'll all help, I think we can get there."

Paisley passes out nomination forms, and cards with the website URL where they can submit nominations once they've left tonight. "Thank you all, and please feel free to call me with any questions. My phone number and email address are both on that card, below the website listing. I try to reply as promptly as possible during the holiday season. I don't want details to impede our desire to bless these children."

Pais and I each take a door and people hand us nomination forms on their way out. Once the last person waves and walks out the door, I lock it behind her and blow out all but one of the Christmas Cookie candles. Paisley and I buckle down to work immediately, compiling a list of people to contact. A few people added names to the volunteer column as well, and my heart swells. Several others indicated they'd be willing to sponsor more than one family.

"We're almost done with the nominations," I tell her. "Why don't you take the volunteer names and update that spreadsheet for me. I'd love to send out the introductory email tomorrow. We always get a flurry of new sponsors when that goes out, plus maybe you can post our numbers and our mission statement to the Facebook group and hopefully get some shares that way."

Paisley is a whiz with lists of any kind. Sometimes I think she manages lists better than the computer. Whenever I comment on it, she says her parents had her working on lists of things before she could even talk. I've never asked her about her parents, and she's never volunteered much more than that.

"Sure boss, right away."

"I'm not your boss here, Pais. You're a volunteer same as me."

She rolls her eyes. "Except you're the Chair, and I'm still getting paid. But whatever you say, boss." She salutes me.

Paisley hops on the computer with a saucy grin on her face, and the clacking of her fingers on the keys soothes me. After a long and exhausting tax season, it's a relief to be focusing on the one thing I love more than taxes for a few weeks before we start all over again.

"Umm," Paisley says, "I found something a little odd on this list."

I tilt my head sideways. "Odd? What does that mean?"

"Well, I need to compare something first." She walks across the room and peers over my shoulder at the list I'm finishing up of nominated families. "There." She points. "That says Lucas Manning, right?"

I squint at the screen of my laptop and nod. "Yes, Lucas Manning, at 236 Sunset Cove."

"Can the same person be both a nominee and a volunteer?" she asks.

I scrunch up my nose. "No. If they're a legitimate participant in the program, they shouldn't be able to afford to sponsor a family."

Paisley walks back over to the desktop, and I follow. About a third of the way down her list, there's his name again. Lucas Manning, 236 Sunset Cove."

"Gah," I say, "what a mess. We must've included his

name by accident. We'll have to go over the initial forms and figure out which one he really is."

We search and search, but sure enough, we didn't make a mistake. His name and address are listed here on the nominee form, and someone filled his name and address out as a sponsoring family as well.

"Now what?" I wonder out loud.

"Has this ever happened before?" she asks.

I shake my head. "Not that I know of."

"What do we do?"

Take the bull by the horns, I suppose. "I'll call him and set up an appointment to discuss the program. I don't think it's a subject I should broach over the phone, because if he's a sponsor, he'll be offended someone nominated him, and if he's a nominee, he'll wonder if other people disapprove of him taking things as evidenced by his name being listed as a sponsor. What a snarl. Hopefully the answer will be glaringly obvious once I reach his house, and I can play it off as a standard preliminary meeting either way."

"Good idea," Paisley says.

I dial the number listed, and the phone rings and rings. Finally it goes to voicemail. Lucas Manning has a deep voice with a faint accent I can't place, at least, not from hearing only ten words. I leave a message asking him to call me at the United Way office.

Not five seconds after I end the call, my phone rings and the words UNKNOWN CALLER pop up on the screen. Probably Lucas returning my call.

"Wow, that was fast," I say.

"Mary?" My boss Shauna's voice, even just saying my name on the phone, is unmistakable. "What was fast?"

I cringe, not that she can see it. "Your phone number came up as unknown, and I thought you were someone with Sub-for-Santa returning my call." Which was stupid, because I only gave him my office number.

"Ah, okay. Are you busy tonight? I was hoping you could meet me for dinner. I need to talk to you, and it's important."

"That sounds ominous," I say.

She laughs. "Well, we do have a lot of data to review. I got our analyst's reports on numbers and performance for the year."

My stomach turns. "You're not firing me, right?"

"I'd hardly do that over dinner. I'd have to wait until the end of the meal to tell you, which would be beyond awkward when I finally got around to firing you."

She also wouldn't be making a joke about it if it were happening. I relax a little bit. "Where did you want to meet?"

"Bentleys, eight sharp. Dress nice." Shauna hangs up the phone.

"Was everything okay?" Paisley asks.

"I'm wearing black pants and a red sweater. Does this count as 'nice enough for Bentleys' do you think?" It's one of the premiere steakhouses in Atlanta, and I've only been once.

Paisley scrunches up her nose. "Well, I've never been there, but. . ."

"That bad?" I sigh. "Shauna wants to see me, and she said to meet her there. She reminded me to dress nice, like I need someone to tell me how to pull my pants on the right legs."

"Bizarre. Although you are her rising star. Probably just another client that asked for you specifically. If she's giving you more work, I know it goes against every part of your character, but you need to demand a raise. You already work harder than everyone else in that stupid office."

I wish. "No way is she calling me over to give me a raise. In any case, I have forty-five minutes until I'm supposed to arrive, and it's fifteen minutes to get to my house for a change of clothes. Bentleys is a solid twenty minutes away from home. I'm sorry to ditch you, but I better run."

"I have a cocktail dress in my trunk. If you ask nicely, I might be persuaded to share."

I raise one eyebrow. "Do I even want to know why you have a dress in the back of your car?"

She grins. "I'm single, and I like to be prepared. You never know where the night may lead."

I always know where mine will go. My nights beeline toward a TV dinner in front of an episode of Gilmore Girls. But that's kind of pathetic. I should have a cocktail dress in my trunk. I should be spontaneous and fun.

"I'm single too," I say, "and the only thing in my trunk is dust bunnies, hiding amidst old tax files."

"You want the dress, or not?" she asks.

"I might. Lemme see it." I follow her out to her car.

She lifts the trunk and slides a black bag out. She pulls the zipper down to reveal a blood red sheath dress with black piping. I gasp. "Yes, I'd love to wear that, but I doubt it'll fit me."

Paisley eats like a bird and it shows, but one quick try on won't hurt. If by some miracle it fits, I'll spare myself a lot of anxiety about traffic and changing in time to reach Bentleys.

Paisley snorts. "It'll look better on you than on me I imagine, especially with your coloring. I mean come on, this vibrant red with your blonde hair and hazel eyes? Not to mention your golden tan. Remind me why we're friends again?"

I don't bother correcting her, but my skin isn't actually tanned. My dad's half Italian, so my skin's darker than your average white person.

I roll my eyes. "Obviously I've been using you this whole time for the day I would need a cocktail dress with no notice."

I leave the conference room and walk around the corner to try on the dress in my office. Paisley stands guard by my door just in case. It's late enough that everyone who normally works here is gone, but I'm not taking any chances on janitorial staff. The dress is red satin, with panels that alternate between shiny and matte in vertical stripes. It's a little snug, which means it shoves my chest up near my collarbones.

"I don't think I can go out in public looking like this."

"You have to at least show me," Paisley whines. "Come on, lemme see it. I have no exciting news, so I need to live vicariously."

I step out of my office.

Paisley whistles and claps. "If you were going on a date instead of to meet our boss, I'd totally force you to wear that. Since it's just a work thing, it's your call. You're welcome to borrow it as long as you dry-clean it afterward."

I bite my lip while I think about it. "It will be way easier than trying to drive home first, so I'll borrow it if you're sure it's okay."

She nods. "Totally fine."

"Thanks." I slide into my boring black pumps and grab my purse. "Actually, I should probably use the time I'm saving to help you finalize the nominee list."

Paisley shrugs. "I can finish the last few up here, no problem. Order the most expensive thing on the menu. Frank & Meacham owes you a nice meal for coming in on no notice, and late at night. Not during tax season." She scowls. "Those guys abuse your work ethic."

"I'll order the lobster and the steak."

"Oh man, then bring me leftovers. And to pay me back for the loan, text me and let me know what's going on. I love firm gossip."

"Will do." I pull my light brown leather jacket on over the stunning red dress, and walk out the door.

I run through a list of things Shauna might need to tell me. It can't be a promotion, because I'm a senior associate, which means she's got the only position above mine. I can't imagine she'd fire me. My hands shake. Could she be transferring me? There's a rumor going around that the London office is struggling. I can't leave my baby sister Trudy here in Atlanta alone, and she'd never follow me to London. If that's it, I'll have to tell her no. Can I tell her no?

I'm deep in thought, and only a few steps away from the comfort of my Honda Accord when I bump into someone.

My heart accelerates and I stumble backward, blinking my eyes in the cold air to help focus them. Strong hands wrap around my upper arms, steadying me. "Mary?"

I look up into the face of my ex-fiancé, Foster Bradshaw. He looks every bit as aristocratic and perfect as ever. I shouldn't be surprised to see him here, since he runs United Way's Atlanta office, but he's not usually here after hours. His dark hair falls softly over his forehead and ears. His deep blue sweater exactly matches his eyes. He knows it, too. With Foster, nothing is ever a coincidence.

"I'm so sorry, Foster. I didn't see you."

"Obviously." The humor in his tone rubs me the wrong way, or maybe it's my body's reaction to his cologne that makes me cranky. "Do you have a few minutes to spare? I need to talk to you about something."

Get in line, buddy. "Sorry, I don't actually. I just got a call from my other boss, the one who pays my bills. I've gotta run."

"Always working, even after tax season has ended. Typical Mary. Well, don't let me stop you, but I'd love to touch base sometime in the next few days before things get crazy." He releases me and steps back. "Be careful. It's icy out there."

I practically sprint to my car. Whatever my boss has to say, it can't be worse than spending another second with Foster.

***

Did you enjoy that? You can grab Finding Faith now for free!

ACKNOWLEDGMENTS

Thank you to my husband, my kids, and my family and friends. They are always so supportive while I write, and understanding, too.

Thank you to my editor, Carrie. She's the best! And to my cover designer, Shaela. Blue Water Books is always amazing!

And mostly, thank you to my fans. Without my readers, I wouldn't be able to do what I love doing.

Bridget's a lawyer, but does as little legal work as possible. She has five kids and soooo many animals that she loses count.

Horses, dogs, cats, and so many chickens. Animals are her great love, after the hubby, the kids, and the books.

She makes cookies waaaaay too often and believes they should be their own food group. In a (possibly misguided) attempt at balancing the scales, she kickboxes daily. So if you don't like her books, maybe don't tell her in person.

Bridget is active on social media, and has a facebook group she comments in often. (Her husband even gets on there sometimes.) Please feel free to join her there: https://www.facebook.com/groups/750807222376182

* 9 7 8 1 9 4 9 6 5 5 6 8 1 *